SEALS
1
AMBUSH!

STEVE MACKENZIE

AVON
PUBLISHERS OF BARD, CAMELOT, DISCUS AND FLARE BOOKS

SEALS #1: AMBUSH! is an original publication of Avon Books. This work has never before appeared in book form. This work is a novel. Any similarity to actual persons or events is purely coincidental.

AVON BOOKS
A division of
The Hearst Corporation
105 Madison Avenue
New York, New York 10016

First Avon Printing: July 1987

AVON TRADEMARK REG. U.S. PAT. OFF. AND IN OTHER COUNTRIES, MARCA REGISTRADA, HECHO EN U.S.A.

Printed in the U.S.A.

K-R 10 9 8 7 6 5 4 3 2 1

AMBUSH!

1

Navy Lieutenant Mark Tynan, a tall, thin man with dark hair and camouflage paint smeared on his face, crouched in the soft, knee-deep, mud and listened to the sounds of the jungle around him. In the pitch black of the tropical night, he could see almost nothing, including the six enlisted men who were hidden in among the trees and bushes that lined the slow-moving river to the south and east of Saigon, close to the South China Sea.

Slowly, like a man crippled with arthritis, he moved his left hand to his cheek to brush away the insect that was crawling there. He had spent weeks telling the six men with him that no movement, for any reason, would be tolerated once the ambush was set, but the night was so dark and his motion so slow that he knew no one would have seen it. Carefully, so that he didn't smear the camouflage paint spread over his face, he flicked the bug to the shallow water that was lapping at his crotch, making his whole existence more miserable by the second.

Tynan dropped his hand again and felt for the mike of the PRC-25 he wore on his back to make sure it hadn't shifted. Then he reached out and gripped the front of the CAR-15. The thumb of his right hand rested against the selector switch, which he had slipped from safe to single shot as he set his ambush.

To his left, on a rotting log that gave a little cover, Tynan had set three flares. Two of them would provide illumination if he needed it, and the third would tell his men, as well as his ship standing a kilometer off the Vietnamese coast, that they were in trouble and had to abandon the ambush site. If that happened, each of the men was supposed to make his own way to the coast to be extracted by a SWIFT boat.

For three hours Tynan hadn't moved, other than to brush the insect. He flexed his muscles, tightening and then relaxing them to keep the blood flowing and to prevent them from cramping as he waited.

He heard jet engines somewhere overhead as American or South Vietnamese planes flew sorties against an unseen enemy. Periodically there was the crump of mortars and the boom of artillery as the fire-support bases fired on suspected enemy patrols or bases. It was all far from Tynan and his tiny group, but it let him know that others were having better luck.

This is one hell of a place for a final exam, thought Tynan. But then, with an elite unit, what could you do? They had trained in the jungles of South America, the Philippines, and Malaysia. They had practiced the art of land warfare with the U.S. Army in the southern United States and worked with the British SAS in Asia. They had fought mock battles against combat-hardened Israelis and even assisted them in an actual raid against Arab terrorists.

With that kind of background, what could you do to really test the capabilities of the new men? Anything arranged would be just one more training exercise and would not be a test of their abilities. Something more had to be done, and that was when Tynan thought of sending them into the swamps and jungles of South Vietnam to mount a real ambush. Let the men infiltrate an area where the VC lived, let them read the signs, if they could find them, and let them organize their position. Tynan would just sit back and let them go, unless they really fucked it up. Then he would flunk them and tell them what they had done wrong, if any of them survived the mistake.

He was wondering if he should pull the ambush out because it looked as if they had picked the wrong place at the wrong time when he heard a quiet swirl of water that sounded as if someone had been too anxious with an oar. He cocked his head away from the sound, using the corner of his eye to search the river because peripheral vision was better at night. But it was too dark to see anything.

Then there was the scrape of wood on wood and a quiet bang of the oar against the side of the sampan. Tynan raised his carbine slightly, pointing it in the general direction of the sound. He wondered what the others were doing, if they had heard anything, but he wasn't going to say a word to them. It was their show.

Just as he saw a shape loom out of the dark, a flash of white from the water against the bow of the sampan, one of the others opened fire with a magazine of tracers. The ruby rounds walked across the stream, splintered into the sampan, and were answered by the muzzle flashes of an AK as one of the enemy returned the fire.

There was an explosion in the center of the stream, but the grenade had fallen into the water and there was almost no shrapnel from it. The other Navy men began to shoot, some with tracers to mark the target and others without.

There was a loud splash, followed by a second, as if someone had fallen out of the sampan. Or had jumped. Firing from the boat ceased at the sound of the second splash.

Tynan and the men with him stopped shooting as well, almost as if someone had passed a command. There was a deafening silence in a world that was black spotted with bright splotches where Tynan had seen the muzzle flashes. He waited for his night vision to return, listening for the sounds of someone swimming. He heard the sampan touch the bank of the stream five or six yards away, but there seemed to be no one in it.

Then, from the other side, there was a burst of automatic-weapons fire from what sounded like an M-16. Tynan assumed that it was the man they had put over there in case the ambush was successful and there was an attempt by the VC to escape into the dark. Tynan made a mental note to tell the guy to use his grenades because they wouldn't give away his position.

There was an answering burst—green and white tracers dancing into the night, followed by the muffled explosion of a Chicom grenade. Tynan turned his weapon on the source of the enemy fire and squeezed off a quick six rounds. Then, with his left hand, he reached for one of the parachute flares. He had already removed the cap so that all he had to do was jam it sharply against his thigh, forcing the firing pin into the propellant charge that fired it.

The flare exploded overhead, bathing the ground in an eerie, dancing, yellowish light that concealed as much as it revealed. Tynan saw the shifting shapes of bushes and trees as the flare swung behind its parachute. Across the narrow stream he could see nothing of the enemy.

He looked to the right, downstream, and saw the sampan. One of his men was working his way toward it, to check it for hidden VC. There was a single shot as the man fired at something in the boat.

Then the flare fell into the water, its light extinguished in a hissing of steam. Again it was dark and there were no sounds near him. Tynan scanned the ground, searching for movement that would betray the VC.

While he waited for something new to happen Tynan checked the flares and grenades in front of him, touching them to make sure they hadn't fallen into the water. Satisfied that they had not shifted, he settled back to begin the wait again. They had had a success, but that didn't mean that the VC wouldn't be running something else down the stream. They might be separated by as much as an hour or more. The next group, if there was a next, might not have heard the firing. Or, if they had, they might send a patrol out to try to discover what had happened. It would give Tynan and his men a chance to ambush another group.

The firefight had lasted less than a minute. Tynan had no idea how well they had done. All he knew was that they had stopped a sampan and there had been two splashes in the water. That could have been bodies falling overboard or it could have been two VC escaping. The man on the other bank might have stopped one or both or neither. The lieutenant would have to wait until the morning to find out. From the position of the stars he thought that sunrise couldn't be more than an hour or so away.

For the next hour, Tynan watched as the stars slowly faded and the sun rose. He listened to the sounds of the swamp and jungle around him and ignored the insects that crawled over him. He was surprised, as he always was, that it could get chilly in the jungle, and with his feet in the water, he was more than just uncomfortable.

As the ground began to brighten, Tynan searched his surroundings, trying to spot his men. Each had found his own cover and moved into it after the sun was down. Now Tynan couldn't see them, though he knew about where they were hidden. He thought he saw one of them adjust a hand, but as he stared at the bush he realized that it was a snake winding its way toward the stream.

When the sun was finally up, Tynan stood, easing his way out of his hiding place to a dry area on the bank. He wanted to sit down and pour the water from his boots and dry his feet, afraid that he would get some kind of foot disease if he didn't get out of the wet socks. But there were still things to be done before he pulled out of the area.

To his right, near the sampan that had six bullet holes in the side facing him, he saw one of the others break cover and begin to edge forward and check it. Tynan slid down the bank, back into the shallow water, and stepped toward the sampan. Inside, he could see the body of a man who didn't wear the black pajamas of a Viet Cong but was dressed in the dark green of an NVA regular. There was no weapon with the body, but it wore web gear and there was a pouch containing extra magazines for an AK-47. The rifle must have fallen overboard during the brief fight.

One of the others appeared, almost out of the ground, and said, "That's one."

Tynan nodded and said, "Check the body for anything that intel might want. Papers, unit insignia, that sort of thing. Be careful, though."

"Yes, sir."

Tynan glanced across the stream and saw the man there moving toward a dark shape lying on the ground.

Although it was light enough that he didn't think the VC would still be out, there wasn't any reason to get sloppy. Besides, the VC did move about during the day when they thought they could get away with it, and Tynan didn't want to get killed because he had made a mistaken assumption.

"You two sweep along the bank here, in both directions, see if anything of interest might have washed up. Watch where you're stepping. I'm going to check on Boone."

With a last glance at the dead man, Tynan slipped into the stream and waded across. The slow-moving water was no real obstacle and came only to his chest at the deepest point. He felt his feet sink deep a couple of times, but by rolling his foot from heel to toe, he was able to free it without trouble.

On the other side of the stream he found two places where it looked as if someone had scrambled out of the water. Tynan knew that Boone had left no traces because to do so would mark his location and he had been careful, but VC fleeing in the night, under fire, wouldn't worry about that. Tynan examined the broken plants, the gouges in the mud, figuring that two people had made them. In one other place it looked as if there might have been a third, or it could be that one of the two had slipped backward, creating the third set of markings. The sampan looked as if it couldn't hold more than three, and one of those was lying in the bottom of it.

Boone, a large stocky man with black hair and large hands, was crouched over the body of another man who was wearing the dark green of the NVA. Near one outstretched hand was an AK-47. A helmet that looked as if it belonged on safari in Africa was lying ten or twelve feet from the body. All the blood seemed to have escaped from the dead man and was floating on the surface of the shallow water that covered the ground.

As Tynan approached, Boone looked up and said, "I think this guy was an officer." He grinned and held up a Russian pistol.

With his foot, Tynan lifted one shoulder so that he could see the collar tabs, but there was nothing distinctive on them. Tynan wondered if the VC removed their rank insignia the way some of the American combat officers did.

"You find anything else?"

"If you mean papers, no. He carried a couple of those lousy Chicom grenades." Boone stood and stretched, as if he had been there for a long time.

Tynan let the body drop back into the water. He looked around slowly, trying to find out what had happened to the third enemy soldier. He was sure that there had to be a third.

Across the stream, he could now see three of the four who should have been there. He whistled once, shrilly, trying to attract their attention, and then signaled them to join him. When he saw they were complying, he turned his attention back to the ground.

Since this was a training mission of sorts, he didn't want to give too much away, but he did want to see if he could find the trail before one of the new guys obliterated it by accident. Tynan assumed that there would be a trail and that it would be close to the body of the second VC.

As he was scanning the ground Sterne stepped close and asked, "We do get credit for the body count, don't we?"

Tynan stared at him for a moment, watching Sterne's brown eyes shift under the scrutiny. When he finally looked away, Tynan said, "What difference does it make? A dead enemy is a dead enemy, and we don't need to count him.''

Sterne shrugged as if to say that he didn't know, but that he had heard about body counts since he was a high school senior and wanted to get credit for everything he did.

''I thought I had taught you that there were more important things than a dead soldier. Documents, for one thing. Prisoners, for another,'' added Tynan.

Before he could go on, Boone said, ''What do you make of this?'' He was pointing to a footprint in the mud, well away from the body and the stream. A brownish splotch of blood was next to it.

''Looks like we've found the third guy,'' said Tynan when he saw the signs. ''What should we do?''

''Follow, I guess,'' answered Boone.

''You guess?''

''Follow and see where it leads,'' said Boone.

''Okay, Chief,'' said Tynan. ''It's your move. You do what you think is right.''

''What's right,'' said Sterne, ''is to call for the PBR and get the fuck out of here.''

''I might add,'' said Tynan, ''that debating tactics in the field is of little value. Not to mention the fact that you've let us bunch up so a smart sniper could take us all out quickly.''

Boone didn't wait for any other encouragement. He pointed to Sterne and said, ''Take the point. You know what to look for. You watch out for the wounded son of a bitch lying in wait. We'll follow him for a couple of hours.''

As Sterne trotted off, looking for a way to penetrate the dense growth that was the major obstacle in front of them, Tynan whispered to Boone. ''It's not a good idea to point in the field. Tends to identify the leaders to those smart-ass VC snipers I told you about.''

Without a word, the patrol moved off, each man taking his position as if it had been assigned to him. Tynan fell back until he was bringing up the rear. The progress was slow because they were trying to follow the trail of the wounded man. They were looking for a freshly bent twig, a new puddle of blood, anything that would suggest that the NVA soldier had passed by.

Sterne didn't like the job of walking point, especially when he knew that there was an enemy soldier somewhere in front of him. But he kept moving forward, taking each step carefully so that he didn't trip a booby trap or, worse yet, give away his position by making noise. His gait was strange, like that of a man whose feet hurt him. His eyes were not on the ground in front of him, but sweeping the trail several yards ahead. He was using all his senses as he traveled. He listened to the sounds of the jungle, the songs of the birds, and the buzz of the insects. On each step he felt the ground with his feet, waiting for a sudden shift in the mud that would indicate a pressure plate. He also waited for the sudden tug at his pants indicating a tripwire. His nerves sang with the constant strain of searching for everything that could kill him.

And to make it worse, there were the snakes. He hadn't seen many since he had gotten to Vietnam. He had been afraid of the cobra because that was the most famous, but he had also been told about the daddy two-step—a snake whose venom was so deadly that you only had time to take two steps before it killed you. He hadn't seen one, but he knew they were out there somewhere.

Suddenly he realized what he was doing. Letting his mind drift, away from the task at hand. He had unconsciously increased the pace, as if it would make the ordeal end sooner. He slowed, then stopped, looking around carefully before he resumed the march. Far to the front, ten or twelve meters, he saw something shiny lying nearly under a bush. He didn't rush toward it, just diverted slightly so that he could examine it.

It wasn't much. Just a piece of metal that could have come from a hundred different things, but the important thing was that it was still shiny. Almost everything would rust or tarnish in hours in the wet, humid environment of Southeast Asia. It meant that the metal had been there for only a short time, maybe only a couple of hours. It meant that they were on the right path.

As Tynan approached, Sterne said nothing. He merely flipped the metal at Tynan and then shrugged, as if to tell him that he didn't know what it was but it seemed to be significant. When Tynan shook his head, telling Sterne he didn't know either, Sterne turned his back and began the search again.

At noon, just as Tynan had decided that they had pushed their luck as far as they could, Sterne halted and then nearly dived to the ground, crawling for the cover of a large bush. Before Tynan could get forward to find out what had happened, he heard the sound of voices drifting to them through the trees and bushes of the thick jungle growth.

Slowly he crawled forward, being careful not to snap a twig or let the leafy branch of a bush whip backward. He placed one hand directly in front of him and slowly eased his weight forward until it was safe to move the other hand and knee. Finally he got down on his belly and inched forward to where he could see a brightness through the foliage.

When he approached Sterne, he halted. Sterne pointed to the front, and through the scattered trees and bushes of the jungle Tynan could see a small VC camp. There were only four structures, mud hootches that were no more than three feet tall and covered with bushes so that the outline of them was hard to see. Two men wearing black pajamas sat in front of one of the hootches, watching a black pot that was in the center of a cooking fire. Another man left one of the hootches, shouted something in Vietnamese to the two men near the fire, and then disappeared into another hootch.

Off to the right was a man in a khaki uniform, holding an AK-47 and staring into the jungle. On a platform stuck in the crotch of a tree, twenty or thirty feet above them on the other side of the clearing, a man crouched. He held an AK and wore black pajamas and a pith helmet that was pulled low as if he wanted to sleep.

Tynan reached out and touched Sterne on the shoulder. When Sterne looked at him, Tynan pointed to the man in the tree, dragging a finger across his throat to tell Sterne to kill him, and then held up both hands, letting Sterne know that he must wait ten minutes before shooting. That done, he turned and worked his way back to where the other members of the patrol waited.

Quickly he filled them in, explaining that there probably weren't more than twelve or fifteen VC in the camp, even if each of the hootches was filled with the enemy. He told Boone to circle to the east, to the side of the camp where the one man watched the jungle, and wait. The others would move forward until they were on line with Sterne, and each would throw a grenade into the camp as Sterne shot the man out of the tree.

Then there was nothing to do but wait a moment. Sterne had eased his M-16 through a hole in the bushes and was aiming at the man on the platform. Tynan rocked to his right and pulled a grenade from his web gear. With the index finger of his left hand, he jerked the pin free, making sure that he held the safety lever firmly in place. Then he got ready to spring to his knees so that he could throw the grenade like a base-ball into the midst of the VC.

To his left, Sterne thumbed the safety off his weapon, took a deep breath and held it. Then he squeezed the trigger slowly, holding the sights of his M-16 centered on the man's chest. There was a single shot that frightened the birds and monkeys in the trees around them. The man on the platform jerked once, started to fall backward, and waved his arms crazily, trying to regain his balance. Sterne fired again, and the man fell to the jungle floor.

Tynan leaped up, threw his grenade, and dropped flat again. He peered through the trees and bushes, watching as the others did the same. There was a series of detonations along the far side of the camp. The two men at the cooking fire had stood when Sterne fired his first shot, unsure of what had happened. They both turned, looking up at the man on the platform, as the grenades exploded behind them, shredding them with shrapnel and turning them into crimson horrors. One of them took a single step forward, as if con-fused, and then fell to the ground. The other simply collapsed.

At that moment, the weapons of the other SEALS opened fire, raking the enemy camp. Dirt spurted from the walls of the hootches as the high-speed rounds drove through them. There was the momentary chat-tering of an AK from the door of a hootch, but that was silenced by a grenade thrown through the door. The VC staggered from hiding and was hit three times by bullets from M-16s. He spun around, collapsing into the dirt.

Seconds later, all the firing died away. The jungle was silent. There weren't even the cries of the birds or animals. Tynan didn't move for a moment, listening. He was breathing heavily, as if he had just run a long distance, the sweat dripping down his face and trickling along his spine. He got to his feet, standing behind a large palm, his eyes roaming over the camp, looking for signs that someone still lived.

Near the campfire, the two men lay sprawled. One of them had kicked over the iron pot as he died, and the remains of the fire smoked heavily. The other was on his back, most of his head missing. The guard who had been at the edge of the jungle was on his side, the front of his khaki uniform now a bright red. Near his outstretched hand was his weapon. Another man was lying between two of the hootches, his back ripped apart by M-16 rounds. Another was near him, missing an arm and part of his leg. There was no sound except the sizzling of the fire.

Tynan moved forward cautiously, his weapon pointed to the front. Out of the corner of his eye, he saw two of the other SEALS move with him. Boone appeared from the left, out of the jungle, but Tynan waved him back, wanting him to cover from there.

Without a word, Tynan pointed toward the bodies and saw his men peel off to check them. They grabbed the weapons lying on the ground, taking the magazines out of them and ejecting the chambered rounds. Tynan leaned his back against the side of one of the hootches and stared inside. A body was slumped near a tiny wooden table that had thick, rounded, short legs. A knapsack was on the table near the fingers of the dead hand, and there were papers scattered across it and the floor.

Tynan crouched and entered. He moved to the body, touching the shoulder. The body fell back, revealing long black hair and a young, almost childish feminine face. One round had hit her in the throat, a small neat hole going in and exiting the back of her neck. The other had hit her in the center of the chest, between her breasts. The front of her black pajamas was covered with blood. Tynan took time to make sure that she was dead, her unseeing eyes staring at the low-hanging thatch roof.

The papers on the table were all in Vietnamese. The knapsack held others. Tynan glanced at them, then swept them all into the knapsack and left the hootch.

Outside, he saw one of the others holding a dark green knapsack. The man sat on the ground, thumbing through it, unaware of what was happening around him. He looked up as Tynan's shadow fell across him.

"Money," he said. "Lots of it." He held up a banded package of it. "North Vietnamese money."

"Anything else in the hootch?"

"Couple of dead guys." The man held up a Russian pistol. "One of them had this. I captured it."

Tynan saw that the others had finished the sweep. Each of them carried a couple of AK-47s, and one held an SKS. He waved them back into the trees and then walked over to the dead man in the khaki uniform to look at the collar tabs, hoping that he would find a unit insignia, but the man had no identification.

He waved at Boone, signaling him to rejoin the group. When he did, Tynan said, "Take the point. Sweep south slightly, and once we're out of here, we'll see about getting airlift."

"What about the wounded guy?" asked Sterne. "The one from the first ambush."

"No time to look for him now," said Tynan. "Besides, he was probably in one of those hootches and is dead. Boone, let's get going."

* * *

An hour later they crouched just inside a tree line, looking south, across a stretch of soft, spongy ground. Boone had just tossed a green smoke grenade into the open, letting the billowing verdant cloud mark their location for the two Huey helicopters that circled in the distance. Tynan had arranged for the choppers using the PRC-25 and the SOI, which gave the radio call signs and held the current authentication tables.

Over the radio, he heard, "ID green."

"Roger, green," responded Tynan.

As he watched, the choppers turned to the north and began to lose altitude. In moments they had changed from tiny specks, barely visible, to large, insectlike machines that roared out of the sky, their rotor blades popping under the strain of the sudden stop. When they came to a hover, Tynan and his men splashed out toward them, the water lapping at their knees, the rotor wash tearing at them and the surface of the water, soaking them. Tynan held his CAR-15 out in front of him, about shoulder high. He held the knapsack of documents in the other hand, trying to keep it dry. He tossed it in the back of the lead ship, put one foot up on the skid that just touched the water, and lifted himself up into the chopper.

Seconds later, the aircraft had turned 180 degrees and was climbing out rapidly. Tynan leaned against the faded gray padding that wrapped the transmission housing and took a single, deep breath. He wiped the water and sweat from his face and then rubbed his hand on the front of his dirty, stained jungle fatigues.

The crew chief leaned close, pushed the boom mike on his flight helmet out of the way, and yelled over the whine of the turbine and the howl of the wind, "Where to?"

"Nha Be," Tynan shouted back. "That a problem?"

The crew chief smiled and hollered, "No. We like the Navy. They have good food there."

2

The flight to the Nha Be Naval Base was a relatively short one. Nha Be was situated on the Saigon River, to the southeast of the Vietnamese capital, and on a delta area not far from the South China Sea. The helicopters touched down on what looked like a dock that ran out into the widening dirty brown river. There were three other choppers shut down there, none of them belonging to the Navy.

Tynan climbed out of the cargo compartment of the Huey and pointed to the gray building that was visible down a graveled road that was lined with whitewashed stones. He put a hand to his eyes to shade them from the glare of the hot afternoon sun and squinted into the distance. Sterne and Boone stepped close to him, but neither spoke.

Tynan glanced to his left and said, "That should be the supply building. Swing by there and see if you can draw some fresh clothes for us. Then find a spot to clean the weapons and the gear. When I finish with intel we'll figure out what to do from there."

"Yes, sir."

Tynan reached over and took the knapsack full of money from Boone's hand. "I'll have to turn this in too," he said. "Not much we can do with North Vietnamese money anyway."

"But it'd be fun to try." Sterne grinned. "We could try to find a bank in Thailand or Hong Kong that would take it."

For a moment Tynan hesitated, as if considering the idea, and then he said, "No. Somebody would just get mad. Besides, just by getting it we've hurt the VC." He shouldered his weapon, checking to make sure it was on safe, and said, "I'll meet you in about an hour. Back here will probably be the easiest way for all of us."

With that, Tynan took both the knapsacks, the one containing the North Vietnamese currency and the other with the papers he had found with the body of the woman. He started down the street, was passed by a light gray Ford staff car that had tinted glass windows and air conditioning but no pennant for an admiral. He saw the entrance to the dining hall but didn't enter. He made his way along a road that had whitewashed posts and chain that formed a fence to keep the sailors from walking on the grass. Real Kentucky bluegrass, not the elephant grass that choked the plains north and west of Saigon.

It was strange, thought Tynan. On the Army bases around Vietnam, the buildings were lined with rubberized green sandbags. The buildings were either a sandy brown or dark brown. The Navy seemed to take things more in stride. They stayed with the light grays they used on all their other bases in the world, and they didn't worry about sandbags. Maybe they believed they were immune to mortar and rocket attacks.

He found the nondescript building that he knew to house the intel function. There was nothing on the outside to distinguish it from any of the other structures around. He opened the single door and entered. The cool breeze from the air conditioning hit him, almost welcoming him in, He walked down the dim narrow hallway, passing closed doors, until he found the one that he wanted. He hesitated outside, then reached down to turn the knob. He thrust it open and stepped in.

The clerk sitting behind the single metal desk looked up and said, "Yes?"

Tynan let his eyes roam over the room. There were a couple of mismatched chairs to one side. A low table stood between them, containing magazines and newspapers, most of them military publications like *Stars and Stripes* and *Navy Times*. The paneled walls held watercolors of the local area and a couple of captured weapons, including an RPG-7. The clerk sat behind his desk, which held three wooden trays piled with papers, a pen and pencil set, a lamp, and a green blotter.

"I need to see Commander Walker," said Tynan as he entered and closed the door behind him.

"You have an appointment?"

"No," said Tynan as he lifted one of the knapsacks to show the clerk. "But I do have something that he might be interested in."

The clerk stood, walked to the door behind him and to his left, and opened it slightly. He spoke quietly, then stepped back and said, "Go right in."

Tynan entered the inner office, stopped long enough to set his CAR-15 in the corner, out of the way, and then turned and saluted Commander Walker. Walker was a fairly short, rotund man with thick black, wavy hair that was sprinkled with gray. He had massive eyebrows, a round face with a pointed nose, and two small brown eyes. Because of his coarse, dark beard, his chin and cheeks looked as if they had been badly painted black.

Walker returned the salute and pointed at one of the chairs in front of his wooden desk. "Have a seat, Mark. Tell me what you've got."

Tynan set the two knapsacks on Walker's desk. "One of those," he said, "contains several thousand dollars in North Vietnamese currency. The other has documents. We got them from a small camp we ambushed earlier this morning."

"Interesting," said Walker. He lifted the flap of one of the knapsacks and reached in. He rummaged around in it and then brought out two stacks of bills. He counted the money rapidly, looked inside again, and said, "Might be thirty, forty thousand dollars."

"That's right." Tynan smiled. "I figured they were going to use it to pay off some of their informers or their local infiltrators."

"More than likely," agreed Walker. "It's a brilliant plan too. Their people can't spend it unless the VC and NVA win since they can't spend the North Vietnamese money in the south. Gives them added incentive."

Tynan leaned forward and grabbed a couple of banded stacks of bills from the knapsack. "I'll keep these and let the boys have them as souvenirs."

"No problem."

Leaning back in the chair, Tynan said, "What I really wanted to know was what is on those papers."

Walker opened the second bag and pulled out several of the documents. He glanced at the top one, then the second, and said, "Table of organization here that doesn't tell us much." He pointed to one of the names. "This Nguyen is the most common name in South Vietnam. Everybody and his sister is named Nguyen. Unless there is more to go on, this one is pretty well worthless."

"I think you'll find more than just organizational charts in there," said Tynan.

"No doubt about it. Take a while to work through this stuff, though."

Tynan got to his feet. "I really should be getting back to my men, but I would like to know what you find in there. If you can see your way clear to requesting the assistance of my team through tomorrow, we could hit Saigon tonight and see you in the morning."

Walker laughed. "That's a little devious."

"Of course, but my boys deserve a little R and R before we get back to the ship," said Tynan.

"Then consider it an official request. I'll inform your captain. I would like to debrief you and your boys tomorrow at ten. That too early?"

"Ten will be fine," said Tynan. "Thanks."

"You need transport to Saigon?"

Tynan shrugged. "What you got?"

"I think there's a couple of PBRs heading up there in an hour or so."

"No, thanks," said Tynan, shaking his head. "Those riverboats are too slow. We'll grab a chopper and be there in a couple of minutes."

An hour and a half later, now dressed in clean jungle fatigues that contained no insignia other than his lieutenant's bars pinned to the collar, Tynan stood in front of the World's Largest PX at Tan Son Nhut, watching the helicopters jockey for position on Hotel Three. He had been forced to leave his CAR-15 locked in the arms room at Nha Be. He wore a forty-five in a shoulder holster under his fatigue jacket. Boone and Sterne stood close by, reading the poster for the movie theater that was on the east side of the PX. Next to them, Carter, Shannon, and Turner waited while

Arnold bought a bag of popcorn from a sidewalk vendor set up near the entrance to the theater.

"What's the plan of the afternoon?" asked Tynan.

Boone turned and shrugged. "I'd kind of like to see the movie. Haven't been to one in a while. That is, if it's all right with you."

"Hell," said Tynan, "it's fine with me. We're off until tomorrow, so if you want to see the film, go. I think I'll head downtown."

"I'll ride along with you, Lieutenant," said Sterne. "That is, if you don't mind."

"Not at all. Any of the rest of you want to come along?" asked Tynan.

Carter and Shannon shook their heads. Carter added, "I'm going into the PX and see how much money I can spend."

"Fine," said Tynan. "Just remember that we have a briefing tomorrow at ten. I'll expect you all to be there. If I don't see you before then, have fun and don't get into any trouble."

"Hell, Lieutenant," said Arnold. "How can we have any fun without getting into trouble?"

Without another word, Tynan turned and headed toward the gate that would let them into Saigon itself. At the gate they caught a taxi, a French car that was almost unrecognizable as a Citroën and was so old that it didn't seem to have a color. Sterne opened the back door and then let Tynan enter. He climbed in after Tynan and asked, "Where we going?"

Tynan leaned forward, glancing into the front seat. He looked at the odometer, which registered kilometers. He couldn't believe that the car had only traveled about ten thousand kilometers and wondered how many times the odometer had turned over.

To the driver he said, "Take us to the Oriental Hotel."

The driver nodded and said nothing.

Sterne asked, "Why the Oriental?"

"We can go pick on the journalists. Let them tell us what we're doing wrong and how we can win the war. Tell them a bunch of lies and see if we can get our names in the paper. Besides, the restaurant on the roof serves good food."

"I had something a little more dashing in mind," said Sterne.

"Well, this is not a mandatory formation," said Tynan. "You're welcome to find your own fun."

"Then I'll let you drop me on To Do Street."

"I'll just give you two pieces of advice," said Tynan. "Watch your mouth and your cock. Don't drink their tiger-piss beer, and be careful with the girls. They'll roll you as quickly as screw you."

"I should be able to take care of myself," Sterne said.

"I'm sure that you can." Tynan leaned forward and said to the driver, "Pull over on To Do Street and stop for a moment."

When the cabdriver complied, Sterne got out and then leaned back to say, "I know about the briefing."

"See you then."

A few minutes later the cab pulled up in front of the Oriental. Tynan got out, haggled with the driver for a minute, and then paid for the ride. He went inside, thought about getting a room in the hotel, and decided against it. If he wanted to stay there, he could always rent the room later. He passed the desk flanked by two gigantic marble pillars, crossed the expanse of worn blue carpeting, and took the elevator to the rooftop restaurant.

He had been sweating from the humidity and heat during the cab ride, but he cooled off rapidly once inside the air-conditioned hotel. As he stepped onto the rooftop restaurant, he was hit with the heat again. The restaurant had huge French doors opening onto a patio that overlooked Saigon. Ceiling fans rotated in the restaurant proper but did little to alleviate the tropical afternoon. A bar stood in one corner and was packed with people. Tables were crammed into every available foot of the floor and spilled out onto the patio and over the rooftop. Potted plants formed a miniature jungle both inside the restaurant and outside. Overhead lights blazed even though the sun, now getting low toward the horizon, still bathed the room in its golden glow.

Tynan shouldered his way into the bar, stepped close to it so that he could shout at the overworked bartenders. He asked for a beer, decided that he didn't want to leave the choice to the man there, and added, "Heineken."

When he got the beer, he pushed his way out of the crowd and looked for a table. He didn't want to sit in the restaurant; it was too hot and too crowded and there was no breeze. He worked his way through the French doors, found an unoccupied table near the wrought-iron railing, and sat down so that he could look at Saigon.

It was a city of sharp contrasts. There were wide, palm-lined streets that were filled with traffic ranging from thousands of bicycles to luxury limousines. Beautiful buildings decorated the city. The Presidential Palace was just that—a palace. Near it was a cemetery containing the bodies of hundreds of French soldiers who had died in Southeast Asia. Both were surrounded by high fences, a couple of tanks apiece, and other, modern buildings.

On the other side were the dirt streets that turned into rivers of mud when it rained. Shelters made of discarded cardboard that disintegrated in the monsoons filled the area. Thousands of tired, dirty people lived there selling anything and everything, and even armed South Vietnamese soldiers had to be careful there.

Tynan sipped his beer and watched the traffic ebb and flow. There was a nearly continuous roar of jet engines overhead, punctuated by the popping of rotor blades and the crash of distant artillery. At the present, none of it threatened Saigon, but Tynan knew that mortars and rockets could be directed into the heart of the city at any moment.

The men and women around him seemed to notice none of it. Most were dressed in civilian clothes and worked in the American Embassy or for the U.S. government. Some of them might have been military, as suggested by their short hair and ill-fitting civilian attire. At one table a brown-haired woman sat with three men, all in civilian clothes. Tynan took another look at the woman. She was tall and slender. Her hair hung well below her shoulders and had bangs that brushed her eyes. She wore a brightly colored sundress, and he could see that the skirt was short.

She turned slowly to him and looked directly into his eyes. Rather than look away, Tynan raised his beer in salute. She smiled and nodded.

A Vietnamese waitress appeared at his side and asked if there was anything that he would like. She stood poised like a vulture waiting for its prey to die.

Tynan was going to shake his head and then decided to eat. He said, "I would like a steak, rare, baked potato with butter but no sour cream, and any green vegetable you might have, steamed rather than boiled."

The waitress nodded and left. Tynan looked back, but the table where the woman had been was empty. He caught a glimpse of her as she disappeared through the French doors into the restaurant. For an instant he thought about following, if only to ask her name, but he hesitated too long and she was lost in the crowd.

Instead of worrying about it, he ordered a second beer as the waitress made her rounds and sipped it, watching the colors in the sky fade from bright blue to reds and oranges and finally into deep purples. Below him, the streets brightened as the neon of a hundred bars and nightclubs advertised their presence.

Tynan ate slowly, once his meal was delivered. He savored the richness of the steak, barely held over the fire so that the outside was charred but the inside was juicy and tender. The butter in the baked potato melted into rivulets that ran down the skin. It was the best meal that he had eaten in quite a while, although the Navy historically had good food. This was more than good; it was great.

He had just finished the last of the steak and pushed the plate away from him when he glanced at the French doors. The woman stood there, as if searching the terrace for someone. On a whim, Tynan raised his hand and called, "I'm over here."

The woman turned, surveyed the tables on the roof-top slowly, and saw Tynan. Surprisingly, she waved back and started toward him.

As she approached his table Tynan stood. He wasn't sure what he was going to do, but he figured the opportunity was too good to pass up. When she was near, he moved so that he could pull a chair out for her and said, "Glad you could make it back."

She sat down, slid her chair closer to the table, and said to the waitress who appeared almost magically at her side, "I would like a glass of red wine." Then she smiled, revealing even white teeth. She had deep blue eyes; Tynan had never seen eyes so blue.

He sat down and looked at the woman. Although it was now evening, she hadn't changed clothes since the last time he had seen her. She still wore the sundress with the short skirt that barely reached to mid-thigh. It was cut low in front, and Tynan could see sweat beading between her breasts.

He sat there for a moment, staring at her, wondering what witty thing he could say to impress her but coming up with absolutely nothing. He felt the ease of the silence disappear and become tense. He wanted to fill it with sound of some kind, so he asked, "You come here often?"

The waitress delivered the wine and faded into the approaching night. The woman tasted her drink, smiled, and said, "I'm here almost every night. It's about the safest place around."

"Because the rockets and mortars land more in the center of Saigon?"

"No, because most of the military people hang around To Do Street," she said, smiling again. "You're one of the exceptions, although I see you're in the Navy."

"Now how in the hell did you know that?" asked Tynan, aware that his jungle fatigues only revealed that he was in the military but not which branch.

She pointed at his collar. "Your lieutenant's bars are the kind worn by the Navy. The connecting piece on them is on the end and not on the sides."

Tynan laughed, genuinely impressed. "That's very good. I'll bet not one person in a hundred would have noticed that."

"I also noticed that you wore no other insignia. If you had been a Marine, you would have had the birdie on the ball displayed somewhere. Only conclusion I could draw was that you are in the Navy. You stationed in Saigon?"

"No. I'm attached to a ship that is standing off the coast right now. Managed to convince a number of people that I should be on shore for a night." Tynan leaned forward, his elbows on the table. "And you?"

"Nothing spectacular, I'm afraid. Have a job in the American Embassy and have to get away from it and the embassy crowd once in a while. See how the other half lives." She wiped a hand across her forehead and looked at the sweat on her fingers. "Sure doesn't get cool in the evenings, does it?"

"Never does in the tropics," said Tynan. "I hate to seem forward, but you haven't told me your name."

"It's Susan Harris," she said, holding a small hand with slender fingers across the table. "But everyone calls me Bobbi. That's with an *i*."

Tynan shook her hand and said, "That doesn't make a lot of sense—Bobbi with an *i*."

"My middle name is Barbara and there were four Susans in my class in school, so we started using our middle names, and Barbara is just too formal for a little girl."

"Well, I like it," said Tynan.

"Bobbi or Barbara?"

"Both," said Tynan. "Or Susan, for that matter."

"Well, thank you, I think," she said.

Tynan glanced at the restaurant. He could see a live band playing, heard it too, and saw that a few people were dancing near the bandstand. Several couples were on the rooftop dancing under the stars. Beyond them, in the distance, Tynan could hear the rumble of artillery. Closer in, he could see a parachute flare rocking toward the ground.

For a moment he sat there, staring at the flare, wondering what was going on below it. Then he turned his attention back to Bobbi Harris. "Would you care to dance?" he asked.

"On one condition," she said. "You have to tell me your name."

"Tynan," he said. "Mark Tynan."

"Well, Mark Tynan, I would love to dance with you." She stood up.

As they moved toward the open area where the others danced, Tynan asked, "Aren't you waiting for someone else? You looked like you were searching for someone when you came back."

She took his arm in both her hands. "I was. I was looking for you."

"Me? You don't even know me."

She stopped walking and turned so that she could look deep into his eyes. "I know that. But I saw you sitting by yourself. You seemed so different from the men I see around here. I just wanted to get a chance to talk to you a little bit. I had hoped that you hadn't left, and you hadn't."

"You don't waste time," said Tynan, thinking that the roles had somehow become reversed.

"There's not a lot of time to waste," she said.

At ten o'clock the next morning, Tynan was sitting in Commander Walker's office, waiting for one of Walker's assistants to arrive. The other members of the patrol were there too, sitting in folding chairs brought in for the purpose. Sterne looked as if he hadn't been to bed, or rather to sleep. His uniform was dirty and torn, and there was a large bruise under his eye. He just said that it was from having a little too much fun on To Do Street.

The others apparently hadn't had as much fun as Sterne. They were all fairly clean and looked like they had gotten some sleep. Tynan noted that they were there and then thought about Bobbi Harris. She was quite a woman.

Walker interrupted his train of thought by opening the door. "This is Chief Petty Officer Eric Braden," he announced. "He'll brief us on the documents you men found for us."

Braden moved so that he was standing near the edge of Walker's desk. He set a file folder, stamped top and bottom with red SECRETs, on the corner. Braden was a tall, skinny man with thick black hair and a bushy beard. Navy regulations allowed sailors to have neatly trimmed beards, but Braden had let his get away from him. It nearly obscured his face.

"Gentlemen," he said in a high voice, "the documents you found proved to be very interesting. We haven't had the chance to scan each one carefully and in detail, but we have formed a few preliminary conclusions."

He stopped talking, opened his folder, and said, "The information I'm about to give you is classified as secret and must not be discussed outside this room or with anyone not cleared by Commander Walker's office. Is that understood?"

When he saw everyone nod or heard them respond, he said, "Good. Now, first, we have a list of many of the agents that are being used by the local VC to gather information. By that, I mean that we know who is working on the American installations and what they are doing for the VC. You know—searching for the ammo dumps, fuel storage, arrangement of the aircraft on flight lines, arms lockers, that sort of thing. Just exactly what you would expect an enemy agent to be looking for. No surprises, other than a couple of the names. Those people are either being arrested or are now under surveillance."

He flipped through a couple of papers and said, "The real interesting stuff is a plan to hit Fire-Support Base Crockett with a reinforced regiment. The attack is scheduled to begin in two weeks, give or take a couple of days. They want to overrun a fire-support base to prove that they can do it.''

Tynan clapped his hands together and said, ''The Army will be glad to hear that. Give them time to prepare for the enemy assault.''

''That really won't be necessary, Lieutenant Tynan,'' said Walker.

''What do you mean?'' he asked.

''The Army doesn't need any warning. The VC can't take a fire-support base. Do you know what that is? An artillery battery, either one-oh-fives or one-five-fives, surrounded by two or three infantry companies, and each base is in firing range of three or four others that can lend support,'' explained Walker.

''That doesn't mean that we can't tell them that the attack is coming.''

Braden took over. ''Lieutenant, these documents haven't been fully evaluated. We don't know how valid the information contained in them is. Right now the consensus upstairs is that this plan to overrun a fire-support base is just wishful thinking on the part of the VC.''

''That still doesn't mean that we shouldn't warn the Army,'' said Tynan. ''Hell, tell them the same thing that you told us. Tell them that you don't trust the information but you thought they might like to know it.''

''Let's finish the debriefing,'' said Walker. ''Chief, go ahead.''

''Yes, sir. The plans were fairly detailed,'' he resumed, ''giving the order of battle of the battalions to be employed and a schedule for the assault.'' Braden smiled. ''A wonderful work of fiction.''

For the next hour they went over the rest of the documents. They contained a plan for a mortar attack on a Special Forces, plans for a weapons buildup south of Nha Be, descriptions of American arms, and a manual on how to care for the M-16 with Vietnamese translations on the side. Most of it was fairly mundane, almost uninteresting, except for the source. Finished with that, Braden asked each of them to describe what he had seen during the mission and what had happened during the assault on the enemy camp. Was there anything unusual about the men in the camp? Did they seem to be well trained? Anything that might not have been mentioned?

When Braden was finished, Walker told them all they could head back to their ship. As they moved to the door Walker added, "Lieutenant Tynan, I would like to see you for a moment, alone, if you please."

When everyone was out of the office, Walker said, "Close the door."

Tynan complied and turned to wait.

"I want to make sure that we understand one another," said Walker. He sat down behind his desk, picked up a yellow pencil, and held it between his hands. "The information we have is not to leave this room. If I decide that the Army is to get it, I will inform them, but until that time, no one says a word about it. Understood?"

Tynan shook his head. "I'm afraid that I don't," he said. "Why delay?"

"Because we don't have proof that it is going to happen. If we call the Army and tell them and there is no attack, it's going to make us look like a bunch of idiots. If we wait until we have some confirmation and then tell them, we'll be in much better shape."

"That makes no sense," said Tynan.

"Then let me explain it this way. The Army won't lose a fire-support base. The VC can't take it. That is a given. Now, if we tell them we suspect an attack, they're not going to do anything anyway. If the attack doesn't come, the Navy looks bad. Looks stupid.''

"So we say nothing about it and the Navy looks good," said Tynan.

"Not quite as simple as that. We'll work on confirming the information, and if we find that it is valid, then we'll alert the proper officers over at MACV. Right now we just sit quietly and pretend we know nothing.''

Tynan reached for the doorknob. "Is that all?"

"Just so we understand one another, Mark. You are not at liberty to discuss this."

"Yes, sir."

3

Mark Tynan sat on the bunk that was bolted to the bulkhead in the tiny room that was the quarters he shared with an ensign while he was on ship. He had his back against the wall and the heels of his boots hooked on the metal frame of the bunk. He riffled through the stack of North Vietnamese money a third time, letting the breeze caused as he flipped the bills play across his face. The final tally had been closer to a hundred thousand dollars, not the thirty or forty thousand Walker had estimated when he inspected the satchel of cash. Seven VC and NVA men and women with nearly a hundred thousand dollars and plans to overrun Fire-Support Base Crockett.

He tossed the bills at the small writing desk that could fold up into the bulkhead. The whole thing made no sense, but the worst part was Walker's refusal to even consider warning the Army. Tynan knew that Walker was right about the Army being able to repulse any assault made by the VC and the NVA, but it seemed that a warning would give the Army an added edge.

The knock on the bulkhead brought him out of his reverie. He sat up, let his feet drop to the deck, and called, "Come!"

Paul Duke, the NCOIC of Tynan's regular team, slipped the curtain aside and stepped in. Duke was thirty years old and had been in the Navy since he was eighteen. He was just six feet tall and had wavy black hair. He had a barrel chest and large hands. He looked as if he could crush another man if he wanted to.

"Yes, Paul," said Tynan. "You got something on your mind?"

"Yes, skipper, I sure do. We haven't talked about the training mission yet. You were gone an extra day."

"The mission was fine. Everyone did a bang-up job. The problem was not with the men who went out but with the Navy in Nha Be."

"Yes, sir."

Tynan pointed at the chair in front of the desk. "Sit down, Paul, and I'll tell you all about it."

For the next thirty minutes Tynan told Duke everything about the mission and what they had discovered. He got up to pace, which was difficult in the tiny cabin, stopping once to hold up the North Vietnamese money. When he finished, he sat down again and stared at Duke.

"So what are we going to do?" Duke asked. "We can't leave it at that."

Tynan nodded his agreement. "That's what I've been thinking. Walker said they wanted more information before they tell the Army anything. I was thinking that we should get it for him."

"Which means?" asked Duke.

"Simple. If the VC are building up around Fire-Support Base Crockett, there is going to be a lot of evidence of it. I would think that a recon through the area would turn up the proof that Walker demands."

"Yes, sir," said Duke, rising. "You want me to round up the boys?"

"Yeah. Bring in the new guys too. We're going to need all the help we can get on this one."

"Where do you want to meet?"

"On the fantail in about an hour. I'm going to talk to the captain about putting us ashore. Tell him that we've got a few things that we need to iron out."

Tynan found the captain in the wardroom drinking coffee. He was sitting at the table reading an overseas copy of *Time*. He looked up when Tynan entered and said, "Good afternoon, Mister Tynan."

"Afternoon, Captain. You got a minute?"

The captain, a small man with thinning light-colored hair, set his coffee on the table. He had small eyes and a small mouth under a pointed nose. All his features seemed to be squeezed together in the center of his face.

"Sure. What's on your mind?"

"I'd like to put my team ashore again for an extended recon into War Zone C. The whole team this time, including the new guys."

"You think this is necessary? I thought the last patrol was your final exam, so to speak."

"Yes, sir," said Tynan. "Except that it was fairly routine—move into the area during the day and wait. I'd like to do something that would require us to stay in the field for about a week, maybe a little less. That way I can evaluate the men on a number of talents from moving through the jungle at night to setting up camp. I can see if they can maintain tight discipline for an extended time in the field."

"When did you want to go out?"

"Thought that we could redeploy to Nha Be this afternoon and then get Army Aviation to take us into the field sometime early tomorrow."

The captain picked up his coffee and drank. As he set the cup down he asked, "You coordinated this with the Army or our people at Nha Be yet?"

"No, sir, but they have so many people running around that getting a ride into the field is no real problem."

"How do you plan to maintain radio contact?"

"Use the PRC-25. The radio room is set up to monitor that freq."

"Correct me if I'm wrong, Mark, but the range on those isn't all that great."

Tynan rubbed his chin. "No, sir, it's not, but we'll be able to maintain contact with the Army and they can relay messages back and forth."

The captain flipped his magazine closed and stood up, walking over to the coffeepot. "I don't like this. Seems a little haphazard."

"Not really, Captain. Just a standard patrol into the field. Equipment won't take more than an hour to issue and prepare. No route designations because we'll want to operate freely, but a general location can be mapped."

The captain gestured with the pot, pointing it at Tynan. He said, "Check in at six each evening. I'll expect a full written report as well as a verbal debriefing when you get back. When do you want to take off?"

Tynan shrugged. "Figured about sixteen hundred. Chopper into Nha Be."

"I'll arrange that for you. After that you'll be on your own. You'll have to get transport into the field and back to Nha Be. Be sure to coordinate with Walker there. I don't want you fouling up anything that he might have going out."

"Yes, sir. No problem."

* * *

Duke had the men assembled on the fantail. They were sitting in a semicircle, cleaning their weapons. Most of them carried M-16s. Duke had an M-14 and had given Carter an M-79. There was a box of hand grenades next to Boone. A couple of crates of claymores sat next to the grenades, and next to them were four boxes of C rations. Other, loose equipment like spare canteens, extra socks, flashlights with red lens covers, and combat knives was scattered around them.

Thomas Jones, the youngest member of Tynan's regular team, sat by himself, checking the radio and its battery pack. He was eating a Hershey milk chocolate candy bar that he set next to him between bites. As always, his longish blond hair needed combing and he had rolled the sleeves of his jungle jacket up over his biceps. He had a narrow face that was unmarked by wrinkles or pimples even though he ate candy bars as if they were about to be declared illegal.

As Tynan approached he called to Duke, "You get everything we needed issued?"

"Yes, sir. Supply didn't give me their normal ration of shit when I began asking for the stuff."

"Good. You check everybody's pack?"

"I was about to." He turned his attention to the men seated near him. "Okay, boys, open them up and let me look inside." He moved down the line, checking to make sure that each of the men had packed extra socks, a poncho liner, insect repellent, spare ammo, and C rations. He stopped and told Shannon that he needed to take the C rats out of the boxes they were issued in and repack them, throwing away the worthless shit that the bureaucrats in the World thought men in combat would need: tins with two crackers and runny jelly, canned bread, and little gift packs with stale cigarettes, old candy, and chewing gum that was nearly impossible to chew. Each item added extra weight. By throwing away the worthless shit, they could carry other things, such as more spare ammo.

Finished with his inspection, he was pleased with the pile of extraneous material he had found. He was even more delighted with the shocked expressions as he kicked the pile of shit over the side of the ship. He pointed down, toward the azure water of the South China Sea, and said, "That is where most of that crap belongs. Don't carry something you don't have to. Put in an extra pair of dry socks. Nobody realizes the importance of being able to dry his feet once a day."

Duke wiped a hand across his forehead. A couple miles out to sea, the breeze created as the ship steamed along its picket station made the humid tropical sun easier to take. It made the warm afternoon seem almost pleasant.

To the men Duke said, "I've noticed that each of you has a single canteen. That will not do. Three at a minimum. In the field you cannot drink just a portion of the water in the canteen. You must empty it because you cannot go creeping through the bush with water sloshing around."

Turner had used electrical tape to attach his paratrooper knife to the shoulder strap of his web gear. Duke looked at that and said, "Wrong. Wrong. Wrong. You tape it on upside down so that you can draw it easier in an underhanded motion. The way you have it there leaves you wide open. Your belly and chest are unprotected as you reach for it. You don't like that, you tape it to a boot, although that will mean that the blade will get wet and probably rust."

There were suddenly a hundred things that Duke wanted to tell the men, but he knew that he didn't have the time. Little things like taping the excess material of their fatigue pants down so that it wouldn't rustle the leaves of bushes, or taping their dog tags together so that they wouldn't jingle. Or leaving their wallets locked on the ship. Or staying away from deodorants because Charlie had learned to find Americans by the smell of those products. All things that should have been common sense, but things that men going into the field for the first time didn't know. Instead of saying any of it, he moved back, away from the men, and said, "I guess they're ready, Skipper. As ready as they'll ever be."

Tynan stepped forward. He put a hand over his eyes to shade them from the sun. He looked at each of the men carefully, as if taking a mental roll call, and then said, "This will be a standard recon patrol. We'll want to avoid contact but find the enemy. By contact I mean that I don't want to get into a firefight. We find the enemy, we observe, and then we fade into the night just like Charlie does."

He then added, "That does not mean that we endanger one another. If you must shoot to protect yourself or one of the other members of the patrol, you do it. Now, are there any questions?"

Shannon, who had removed his fatigue jacket and was wearing only a white T-shirt, said, "I assume that this is not a training mission."

"You assume correct." He looked at Duke, who nodded his understanding.

"Yeah, Skipper, I see." Duke pointed at Shannon. "Before we leave, you get to supply and get an OD T-shirt. That piece of shit will be visible for a mile at night."

Tynan stood for a moment watching the men. He suddenly wasn't happy about the patrol because he would have liked to train with the men longer, but it couldn't be helped. Then, as he thought of that, he wondered why he was worried. The men had been through the finest training available in the Free World, and they had proved themselves during the ambush. He decided that it was premission jitters.

He said, "I'll be in my quarters for the next thirty minutes. Anyone needs anything, you can find me there."

Duke said, "Yes, sir."

With that Tynan left the men. He walked off the fantail, down a companionway, and forward to officers' country. In his cabin, he took a key from his wallet and opened his locker. Using a second key, he opened a lock box that he had cemented in the corner. He removed a standard-issue Colt 1911A1 .45-caliber pistol and three spare magazines. He also took out the shoulder holster that was in the box and set it on his cot.

Below that was a second weapon, one that was not authorized by the United States Navy. It was a small 9mm automatic, but with a special modification: a short silencer. Tynan knew that the size of the round and the clattering of the slide as he fired the pistol couldn't be completely quieted, but it would be reduced. The silencer would probably blow itself up before he could fire a full magazine through the weapon, but it did give him an additional edge. By using hollow points he increased the efficiency of the round. The only problem was that the pistol was illegal. Hollow points were not to be used in the war because they were inhumane. The Geneva Convention had dictated that. Tynan smiled at that because he could think of no humane way to kill someone.

And, of course, the silencer was also illegal, although he knew that snipers could use them. The rules of land warfare as applied to Vietnam made little sense. Shotguns were not allowed in combat but could be used to quell riots in Saigon. Willy Pete—white phosphorus—was not to be used as an antipersonnel weapon, but napalm was.

He shook his head to clear it of the thoughts. He had other things to worry about. He took off his fatigue jacket long enough to slip on the shoulder holster for the forty-five. Then he used a specially designed rig that fitted into the small of his back to hold the silenced nine-millimeter. He couldn't draw it quickly but he could get to it, and a hasty search by an inexperienced captor might miss it, though he doubted it.

He checked his watch and saw that it was getting close to the time the chopper was to arrive. He shoved his personal gear back into the wall locker and slammed the door, locking it. He grabbed his equipment, his pack, and his CAR-15. It had originally been designed as a survival weapon, but the Army's Special Forces had found it to be very useful in the close quarters of jungle fighting. Tynan found it to be reliable, especially since the one he had didn't have the standard Army modification that reduced the cyclic rate of fire. That was what caused the weapon to jam. Tynan could burn through his ammunition about two hundred rounds a minute faster than the Army could.

He went back up on deck and turned aft, toward the fantail, where the helipad was situated. In the distance he could see a single Army chopper dropping from the sky as it approached the rear of the ship. The noise from the dual rotor blades and twin engines was already overpowering. Tynan joined his men, who either stood around just off the pad or sat on their packs.

The Chinook slowed as it neared the ship until it was nearly hovering over the fantail, the wash from the rotors whipping across the deck like the wind of a typhoon. Anything that was light and loose was sucked up and blown away. The men turned their faces away, holding their hats on their heads so that the chopper wouldn't snatch them. For nearly thirty seconds the Chinook hovered three or four feet above the pad, seeming to rise and fall as the ship rocked in the swells and troughs of the sea, as if timing the motion. Then, like an overweight turkey, the chopper slowly settled, the speed of the rotor wash increasing. The ship rose to meet the wheels, brushed them, and dropped away. The pilot, apparently believing that he was on the deck, slammed the collective down, reducing the lift of the blades, and the chopper fell nearly three feet, bounced, and sank to the deck.

"Christ," yelled Duke over the noise of the engines and the popping of the blades, "I don't know if I want to fly with this guy."

"Don't worry about it," Tynan shouted back. "Dry land doesn't move around. He knows where it is, and I assume that he can hit it."

"I still don't know," said Duke, shouldering his pack as the rear ramp of the Chinook began to lower.

The crew chief, wearing jungle fatigues and a flight helmet that had a long cord running from the side back into the belly of the chopper, appeared. He held a tiny black box with a single button on it in one hand. He waved to Tynan and his men, then pointed into the interior of the helicopter as if to hurry them into it.

"Let's go, boys," said Tynan as he led them into the helicopter. The interior was dark because there were only a few small, round portholes along the fuselage. There were canvas seats along the sides with red webbing climbing upward from there. The center of the helicopter was stacked with boxes of supplies, everything from crates of ammo to cartons of C rations. These were to be delivered to Army units in the field.

Tynan and his men took seats on either side and buckled in, and before the rear ramp was completely secured, the chopper leaped into the air as if happy to be away from the rocking of the ship.

The noise from the turbines made it impossible to talk inside the helicopter. Tynan sat quietly, wishing that he had brought something to read. He let his mind drift back to the rooftop of the Oriental and Bobbi Harris. They had spent the rest of the evening there, together, dancing and drinking and talking. He could still feel the texture of her bare back as he held her while they danced, a light coating of perspiration heightening the sexuality of the dance.

She had done nothing to deny the growing lust between them. She had held him tightly, gently rubbing herself against him as they danced, breathing an occasional question into his ear, her breath warm and sweet, her voice husky with desire. When he ducked his head to respond, he could smell the perfume on her throat and behind her ear, and the shampoo in her soft hair. She had been trying very hard to get his attention, and she had succeeded quite well.

In what seemed like only moments, the sound inside the helicopter changed and they were descending. They touched the ground, didn't bounce, and then the crew chief was on his feet, again shouting that they had arrived at Nha Be. The men stood, picked up their equipment, and exited. Seconds after they had cleared the rear of the chopper, it was off again, in a swirling storm of dust and debris.

"First order of business," said Tynan, "is to find quarters for tonight, although I suspect the captain will have taken care of that problem. Second is to head over to supply and draw some flares, smoke grenades, and anything else we might need."

"Yes, sir," replied Duke. "And then?"

"We grab chow and some sleep. Tomorrow we hit the field."

4

The day didn't dawn the way Tynan had hoped it would. There were low-hanging clouds threatening rain. There were puddles of dirty water standing in the streets, proving that it had rained the night before, and the humidity hung in the air like the stench from yesterday's dirty laundry. Tynan stood outside the chow hall, staring into the dark sky where the clouds seemed to boil along, watching the shifting shapes turning from gray to black and back again. Just standing seemed to be an effort because of the heat, and he was sweating heavily, the stains spreading under his arms and down the center of his back.

"Going to be miserable out there," said Sterne, who had stopped just behind the lieutenant. "Hot and miserable."

Tynan wiped his forehead with the sleeve of his jungle jacket and stared at the ragged stain there. "Yeah. We're going to have to watch the pace, or we'll all double over with heat cramps or exhaustion."

"What time the choppers going to get here, Skipper?" asked Sterne.

Tynan peeled the camouflaged band off the face of his watch so that he could look at the time. "About thirty minutes," he said.

"I'll warn the others."

"Right. I'll meet you down at the helipads in a few minutes."

Tynan walked back to the room that he had been assigned for the night. Inside, he looked longingly at the six-inch-thick mattress and the clean sheets. There was even a light blanket on the cot because the air conditioning worked more efficiently at night when it didn't have to fight the sun. Tynan pulled the sheets and blanket from the bunk and piled them on the end to tell the hootch maid that he wouldn't be back that evening. Then he gathered his gear, checked his two personal weapons concealed under his uniform, and put on his web gear and pack. Finally he slung an extra bandolier of magazines, each holding twenty rounds, on top of everything else. He grabbed his CAR-15 and headed out the door.

The helipad was a wooden dock that extended out into the Saigon River. Parked at one end of it was a Huey with two bullet holes in the windshield and a third in the thin skin of the engine housing. The metal was peeled back where the round had exited, leaving a fist-sized hole.

Tynan found his men crouched by the side of a gray building, sitting with their backpacks against the wall, their weapons stacked near them. The men looked hot and uncomfortable. Each of them was drinking a Coke as if trying to replace lost body fluids already.

Duke stood off to one side talking to another chief petty officer. Tynan approached, waited for a second, and then said, "Everyone ready?"

"Yes, sir. Spread out the squad equipment so that everyone gets to carry some of it. Shannon has the radio. Boone has the M-79, and everyone has six rounds for it. Got the smoke and flares distributed too."

"Good," said Tynan. He pulled his map out of one of his fatigue pockets. He crouched down and spread the map out. He pointed to an area to the northwest of Saigon. "This whole area is forested. It's not really jungle, but the vegetation does get thick. You could hide a division in there, and I think Charlie has. We'll be working in this location."

Duke nodded. "Yes, sir."

Tynan looked at his men again, realizing that something was odd. Then he understood it. There was a man missing. "Where's Arnold?" he asked.

"Sick. Happened early this morning. He woke up, ran to the latrine, and lost his dinner. I thought that he had just had too much to drink, but that wasn't it. As soon as the sick bay opened this morning, I took him over. Doctor said that it looked like the flu, but they wanted to keep him for observation in case it was dengue fever or something like that."

Tynan nodded. "We couldn't have taken him on the mission even if it was only the flu."

"No, sir, sure couldn't." Duke smiled. "He couldn't decide if he was happy about not having to go to the field or pissed because he didn't get to go."

"You should have told him to be happy. Nothing exciting about going into the field. Here he gets to sleep in air-conditioned comfort, watch TV, and eat real food."

"That's what I told him, but I'm not sure that he bought the whole package. Anyway, he's in the sick bay."

"Did he have any of the team equipment?"

"I split his gear up among the rest of us. Mostly it was just ammo for the M-79 and the machine gun."

There was the sound of helicopters in the distance. Tynan glanced up and saw the two Hueys approaching. He folded the map and said, "I'll want you to take half the men on the second ship. I'll ride on the first. I'll brief the pilots.''

"Yes, sir," Duke said as he turned to face the rest of the men. "On your feet. I want Sterne, Boone, Shannon, and Jones to join the skipper in the first chopper. The rest of you come with me in the second.''

Tynan moved his men away from the second group so that the helicopters would have room to land. Once again he was wrapped in the rotor wash as the choppers flared and hovered and touched the ground. As soon as the skids hit the deck, Tynan was in the back of the chopper, his map spread on the console so that the aircraft commander could see it. Over the sound of the Huey's turbine, Tynan shouted, "Want to land in this area." He pointed to a place that was just north of Trung Lap and southeast of Dau Tieng.

The pilot turned the map so that he could see it better. He pulled the boom mike of his helmet out of the way and yelled back, "That's pretty crummy territory."

"Makes no difference," responded Tynan.

"You got a specific LZ picked out?"

"Anywhere in there will do," said Tynan. "We're making a recon."

The pilot nodded. "Be about a thirty-minute flight. Have some gun-target lines to avoid."

Tynan folded his map and stuck it into his pocket. He moved back and sat on the troop seat that spanned the width of the chopper and was set against the transmission housing. Sterne sat with his back against the post right behind the pilot's seat, his left leg dangling in the air and the barrel of his M-16 pointed down. Boone and Jones also sat on the troop seat, while Shannon sat opposite Sterne, looking out the door on his side of the helicopter.

They lifted off, over the Saigon River, and turned to the west before banking around to the north. They didn't gain much altitude screaming over the swamps and rice paddies south of Saigon. As they drifted toward the west and back to the east, avoiding the gun-target lines that the pilot had mentioned, Tynan could see the smoke and haze that developed over Saigon during the days. Jet traffic buzzed around the southern edge of the city, and there were flights of helicopters popping up all around.

They roared across a two-lane highway that contained hundreds of vehicles from military trucks and jeeps to the bicycles and little Hondas ridden by the Vietnamese.

The terrain changed from the rice paddies and swamps to light scrub and then to forest. Scattered through the trees were more rice paddies and tiny hamlets, their presence betrayed by the metal roofs of the hootches. They began to gain altitude then, rising away from the humidity of the ground to the coolness of the air, but they stopped short, the clouds forcing them back toward the ground.

They flashed past a dozen openings in the trees where they could have landed. Finally, without warning, the helicopter flared and dropped to the ground. The crew chief was leaning around the well screaming, ''We're down. Get out.''

Sterne bailed out the right side of the chopper as Shannon leaped out the other. The men on the troop seat unbuckled their belts and dived clear as the helicopter picked up to a hover and charged forward, toward the trees, before popping upward and over them.

As soon as the helicopters were gone, Tynan was on his feet, running as best he could toward the tree line twenty meters in front of him. The pack bounced on his back, slamming into him with each jarring step, propelling him forward. He ran with his arms outstretched, his CAR-15 in front of him as if he were wading through chest-high water. Then, suddenly, he was among the trees, their dried leaves rattling in the wind that whipped through them. Tynan was sweating heavily and breathing hard even though the run had been less than thirty meters. The humidity seemed to force the breath from his lungs, making him gulp the air, but there was no relief in it. Just more soggy oxygen that formed cotton in his mouth as he tried to breathe.

In seconds the rest of the men joined him and without a word or order they formed a tiny, circular perimeter, each man guarding the earth directly in front of him. Tynan looked around him, saw his men in place, and dropped to the ground, taking his map from his pocket. He spent five minutes trying to orient himself, looking for the place where the dirt road crossed the stream near a big bend in the Saigon River. Nearly due south would be Trung Lap, and a little north of there the remains of a plantation whose owner had refused to honor both government requests for tax payments and VC demands for assistance.

Tynan made his way to Duke, showed him the map, and said, ''Take the point and head about due north until you come to the river, then bend around to the west. If you see anything interesting, hold up.''

They formed up, Duke moving forward quietly, slowly. Jones dropped off to bring up the rear. Tynan and the man with the radio were near the center of the squad as it began winding its way through the trees toward the north. The ground was cluttered with vines and bushes that seemed to reach out and grab at the men. They used their machetes sparingly, not wanting to leave sign for the VC to follow. And they kept the pace slow because of the heat. Even in the overcast, travel across the ground was tiring work. If the sun had been out it would have been nearly impossible for them to move.

They keep going, stopping for an hour at noon to lighten their packs by eating some of the C rations they carried. Tynan hated the boned turkey unless he could salt it, and the salt was supposed to help deal with the heat. When they finished the meal and had buried the remains of it, the cans and cardboard, they moved on, Duke still on the point, still moving slowly.

It was nearly two hours later that he stopped, crouching near a tall coconut that was bordered by two large bushes that were laced with thorns. When Tynan approached, Duke motioned him down and then pointed into the rice fields that bordered the tree line.

At first Tynan didn't understand the significance of what he was looking at. In the fields were nearly forty people planting rice. They ranged from an old man with a long white beard to a couple of young girls who couldn't have been more than twelve. The majority of the workers were young men, just as it should have been.

Except that this was Vietnam and all the young men, and quite a few of the young women, had been drafted or had moved to Saigon or had been killed. Tynan watched the young men, their shoulders wide and strong, and suddenly realized that there were far too many of them.

Overhead, a flight of Hueys flew past, but the people in the rice paddies refused to look upward. Except the young men, who turned their heads so that they could watch the choppers, as if wondering where they were going. One of the men dropped his tool and stood up straight, staring at the flight. Only when it disappeared in the distance did he bend to pick up the wooden fork and begin to work again.

Duke slipped back deeper into the trees and crawled over so that he was close to Tynan. He nodded in the direction of the men and said, "That answer your question?"

"That only tells me that there is a platoon around here. We need to see more."

"Want me to take a couple of men into the field to check ID?" he asked.

"No," said Tynan. "They'll all have ID anyway, even if they are Viet Cong. You'll only tip our hand."

"So what do we do?"

Tynan rolled to his side and got out his map. He studied it carefully but could find no indication of a hamlet or village close by. The notations said that there were numerous villages and plantations in the area. Not much help for his patrol since he already knew that.

"Follow the trees to the north," said Tynan, "and we'll see if we can find anything else."

"Yes, sir." Duke turned and looked back at the rice paddies. "Those boys don't seem to be too happy about working in the fields, do they?"

"No, but it's good cover. Looks like a normal bunch of Vietnamese farmers."

As they pulled away from the rice paddies and began to march north again, the rain started. At first it was just a drizzling mist that obscured the countryside, and then it was a cloudburst with the rain coming down in sheets that threatened to wash away the earth. Tynan called a halt because he could no longer see more than a foot and a half in front of him. He pulled his team close together so that they could see one another and waited for the rain to evaporate.

It was late afternoon when the rain stopped, leaving the ground steaming. Tynan ordered the patrol forward again, still moving north. When the tree line ended, leaving them stranded on the point of a peninsula, Tynan called a halt. He figured that, with a good field of fire in three directions, he had found a good place to rest for a while. Then, sometime before sunrise the next morning, they could cross the open ground for the tree line that was a hundred meters away. He could see that it ran more or less east and west, and that was the direction he wanted to travel.

The men spread out, each staying in the trees, but now on the edge so that they could watch the approaches. Tynan checked his map again and was happy with the progress he had made. As he sat back to eat the applesauce that the U.S. government had supplied with the C rations, he heard the rumble of artillery, but in the distance. He turned but could see nothing. Overhead, a couple of jets roared by, leaving long black trails but dropping nothing.

At six, Tynan used the radio to make contact with an Army Aviation unit that was near, telling them to relay a message to his ship. The code word was *Nabisco,* which meant that they were on the ground and moving and that they had run into no trouble.

When he finished eating, Tynan took off his boots and did his best to dry his feet but didn't use his only pair of clean socks. There was too much time left on the patrol. Having finished that, he relieved Carter, who had been keeping watch while the others relaxed. Carter nodded and smiled and carefully crawled out of the nest he had made for himself at the base of a bush.

In front of him, Tynan saw nothing unusual. Nearly a hundred meters away in a clump of palm and coconut trees stood a couple of mud hootches. In front of them were two cooking fires. Tynan got out his binoculars and scanned the area. There were two young women dressed in black pajamas squatting near the fire. A half-dozen young men were lounging behind them. Tynan could see no evidence of old men or women. Again, too many young men in the area. More evidence of a buildup.

Tynan wondered if he had seen enough. Maybe it was time to turn the patrol around and head for Fire-Support Base Crockett. He could tell the Army commander there that he had seen a lot of military-age men working the fields and living in the hamlets in the Hobo Woods and that he had found a couple of documents suggesting that Crockett was going to be attacked. Scanty evidence at best, but enough for the CO to order an alert.

The sun had fallen so that it was sitting on the horizon, and the clump of trees where the hootches were was wrapped in darkness punctuated only by the flickering of the fires which would soon be extinguished. Tynan searched the trees to the right and left of the hootches and found another fire, but he could see only a couple of shapes silhouetted by the flames. Suddenly he was uncomfortable. There were just too many people wandering the area. Tynan knew that the buildup was taking place. It was slow and it was quiet, and if he could see enough men to make up a reinforced platoon, there were probably four times that number around that he hadn't seen. He had only made a recon of a single day and had found that much. There was suddenly no question in his mind.

His first instinct was to pull camp immediately and try to work his way to Crockett. Then, thinking about it, he realized that the attack probably wouldn't be launched that night. The VC's forces were scattered too far and wide. It would take a day, maybe more, to consolidate the regiment. That gave Tynan the time he needed to warn the Army.

He glanced to his right, but in the fading light of the dying sun and the dense foliage, he couldn't see the man next to him. There was no reason to hurry. They could take a few hours to relax, catch a little rest, and then, about midnight, fall back the way they had come. By morning they would be close to Crockett, and if he felt they had to hurry then, he could always call for airlift.

The ground blackened and the trees and hootches faded from sight. Tynan could hear the noises of the night creatures around him as they moved in search of prey. Overhead was the ever-present popping of rotor blades and the roar of jets. He could hear artillery being fired from one location and landing in another. There was a distant rumbling that could only be the huge bombs from B-52s in an arc light.

In front of him, the fires shrank and disappeared, but he could hear the quiet voices of the Vietnamese as they talked to one another. In the tree line on the other side of the hootches, he saw a light flash once, but it, too, quickly disappeared.

At midnight, Tynan looked at his watch and decided that it was time to get going. He slipped away from the large bush and tapped Duke on the shoulder. In the center of the perimeter they had established, Tynan showed Duke the compass course he wanted to follow, and when Duke whispered that he understood, Tynan added, "We move slowly. I want absolutely no noise. Complete noise discipline. First guy to make a sound gets his butt kicked back to the regular Navy."

They moved out then, Duke in the lead, walking silently, placing his feet carefully so that he made no sound. He used a long pole as a walking stick so that he didn't walk into or off of anything. The progress was slow; after an hour, they had traveled little more than a klick.

Duke stopped when he came to a place where the trees bent back to the west. They either had to detour or to move across open ground.

"It's no problem," Tynan whispered to Duke when he caught up to the point man. "Head across on a straight line. We'll follow but maintain a good distance."

Duke looked upward to where the clouds had thinned until they were nearly nonexistent, letting the moonlight bathe the woods around them. It was no longer pitch black, and Duke could see the palm and coconut trees across the open paddies.

They swept out of the trees, Duke in the lead and the others on his left and right, walking for the safety across the paddies. Tynan stopped when he heard a sound like metal on metal, cocked his head to listen, but heard nothing else. He had taken one step when there was a stuttering burst of fire and green tracer rounds began bouncing through the night.

Tynan dived to his left and landed in the water of a rice paddy. He crawled forward until he was resting on one of the short dikes, staring over the top, trying to spot the enemy weapon. It had stopped firing after the single burst, and Tynan had no idea where it had been.

To the left there was a quiet moaning. Tynan couldn't see who it was. He only knew that one of his men was down and wounded.

He took one of the grenades that he had secured to his web gear and pulled the pin. Carefully, cautiously, he raised up so that he could look at the tree line about forty meters away. He threw the grenade as far as he could, hoping it would land in the middle of the enemy position.

As soon as he released it, he dropped down, keeping his eyes on the trees. There was an explosion, a fountain of sparks shooting upward when the grenade detonated. It was answered by a burst from the machine gun and a couple of AK-47s. This time he saw the muzzle flashes. He had been to the left by a good twelve to fifteen meters.

He crawled to the right, over a dike and into another paddy, trying not to splash the water as he moved. He found Shannon lying on his back in the corner of the paddy, the M-79 cradled in his arms like a baby. Tynan touched Shannon's shoulder, but the man didn't look at him. Then Tynan saw that his eyes were open and staring skyward. A single bullet hole was visible on the left side of his neck just under the jawline. Tynan pried the M-79 from Shannon's nerveless fingers, broke the weapon open, and checked the load.

The machine gun opened fire again, splashing the water of the rice paddies and kicking up the dirt along the dikes, the green tracers lancing through the night and ricocheting into the sky. Still no one on his side opened fire, apparently not wanting to give away their position until they had a better idea about the size of the enemy force.

Tynan crept to the other side of the rice paddy, set the sights on the M-79, and tried to aim at the place among the trees where he had seen the machine gun's muzzle flashes. He fired the weapon and rolled quickly away, back toward the body of the dead Shannon.

There was a pop as the grenade exploded, and there was answering fire from the machine gun. It raked the ground around him, but none of the rounds came very close to him. Tynan grinned at the trees and machine gun and crawled off in the opposite direction. He found Jones crouched in a shallow depression, holding his M-16 in both hands but making no effort to fire it. On his back Jones wore the PRC-25.

When Tynan touched his shoulder, Jones jumped slightly. Tynan leaned close and whispered, "You know what we would do if the situation was reversed? That is, if we caught the VC in the open and had them pinned down?"

Jones shook his head.

"We'd call artillery down on the enemy position and wait until morning to go out and count the bodies."

"Yes, sir," said Jones in a voice that shook only slightly. "So what are you going to do?"

"Call artillery down on those guys and wait until morning to go out and count the bodies." He took the handset from the radio and keyed the mike, saying, "Cu Chi Arty, Cu Chi Arty, this is Black Baron Six."

There was a long delay while Tynan worried that his radio wasn't strong enough to reach the artillery control point or that the rice paddy water had damaged it. Then there was a crackle of static and a barely audible voice saying, "Unit calling Cu Chi Arty, go."

"Cu Chi Arty, this is Black Baron Six. I have contact and a fire mission, over."

"Understand fire mission."

"Roger at X-ray Tango six-two-two-five."

"Understand. Can you spot, over."

"Roger. Can spot. Give me one round of smoke."

"One round smoke." There was a hesitation as the man at Cu Chi Arty relayed the message. Finally he said, "Shot over."

Tynan remembered from his Army artillery class that *shot over* meant a round had been fired. He responded, as he had been taught to do in that same class, "Shot, out."

A moment later there was the rushing of an oncoming freight train that fell to the ground and exploded into a spray of burning debris nearly half a klick to the east of where he wanted it. Tynan keyed his mike and said, "Add one hundred, right five hundred."

The instructions were repeated and then the voice added, "Shot, out."

This time the round exploded much closer to the enemy machine gun in the trees. Tynan said, "Add fifty and right one hundred."

With the second correction, the Willy Pete round exploded right where the machine gun had been. Tynan wanted to stand up and cheer but said, as calmly as he could, "On target. Fire for effect."

Over the radio he heard, "Fire for effect. Rounds on the way."

In seconds there were six explosions among the trees in front of him. Sprays of sparks spurted skyward and filled the night with the buzzing of shrapnel. A few seconds later there were another six explosions, and after that still another six.

Over the radio he heard, "Last rounds on the way."

Tynan acknowledged the transmission and then gave the handset back to Jones. In front of him the last six rounds from the 105mm artillery exploded among the trees. There was the showering of dirt as it rained back to earth. Then there was a sudden quiet as if all the animals around them had been killed in the barrage.

Tynan crawled back to his corner of the rice paddy and opened fire with his CAR-15. The ruby tracers that had been the first five rounds in his magazine laced outward and disappeared into the trees. He waited for several seconds, but there was no answering fire.

Overhead was the sudden pop of rotor blades as two Huey gunships buzzed by, diving at the trees where the artillery had exploded. Neither ship fired and neither was shot at. He heard Jones whispering into the radio, probably talking to the pilots of the helicopters.

"Anyone hurt?" Tynan shouted.

"I took a round in the leg," responded Turner. Tynan easily recognized the voice.

"Bad?"

"I'll live."

"Do you need help?"

"Not right now."

Tynan rolled to his left and got his binoculars from their case. Fires caused by the shelling and the white phosphorus burned in the trees, but even with the added light, Tynan could see nothing other than the trees and the fires. He stuffed the binoculars away and got to his knees. The helicopters flew over again, one breaking to the right and the other to the left, but there was still no shooting from the enemy position.

Tynan, crouching low, ran back to where Jones was mumbling into the radio. As he approached, Jones said, "Gunships are from the Stringers in Cu Chi. Said that they can see nothing moving in front of us."

"Can they stay on station?"

"Gun lead said they would hang around for a while," answered Jones.

"Okay. Let's sweep into the trees and see what we can find." He swung his CAR-15 around and shouted, "On my command, we head for the trees." He waited a second and then yelled for them to move out. A half-dozen shadowy shapes seemed to rise out of the mud and muck of the rice paddies to begin the sweep to the tree line. One of them fired a couple of rounds from the hip, directed at the point in the trees where the machine gun had been.

Tynan walked forward, his nerves on edge, waiting for the return fire of the VC, but it never came. He got closer, sure that he was being watched, and when he was into the trees, he suddenly felt protected, as if the imagined sniper could no longer see him. He turned to the right, where he thought the machine gun had been hidden, but could only find the glowing crater from the artillery. The tiny fires lighting the landscape showed him that the enemy machine gun had been destroyed by one of the 105 shells. He could see part of the trigger housing and a piece of barrel that was still attached to the ruptured feed tray and the bent tripod.

In the darkness he could see no signs of enemy dead, but if the shell had hit close enough to do that kind of damage to the gun, then the bodies would have been torn to shreds and it wouldn't be until morning that they would be able to find anything at all.

He ordered his men out of the trees, and they worked their way back into the rice paddies where Shannon lay dead and Turner was still wrapping bandages around his bleeding calf. The single .30-caliber bullet had passed through the fleshy part of his leg, and although the wound was painful, it wasn't very serious. Duke crouched down, pushed Turner's hands away, and took over the duty of bandaging the wound.

Then they swept back to the trees, on the side of the paddies away from where the enemy machine gun had been, and set up security. Tynan called the Stringer aircraft and told them that the VC either had all been killed or had evacuated the area. He thanked them for their help. That done, and with Turner's wound bandaged, there seemed to be nothing more to do but wait for morning. Tynan ordered half the team to go to sleep as he waited for the sun.

5

Tynan was happy when the sun finally appeared the next morning. The low-hanging clouds near the horizon blew away quickly, leaving the sun alone to bake the scraggly trees and the dwarf bushes of the Hobo Woods. He stared down at the poncho-wrapped body of Victor Shannon, who had endured everything that the United States Navy, the British SAS, and the Israelis could throw at him so that he would have the opportunity to step in front of a Viet Cong bullet before he had much of a chance to play at combat.

Tynan wasn't happy that Shannon was dead, he was just happy that it was morning. Actually, he didn't feel much at the death of Shannon. He didn't feel guilt even though he was leading the men when Shannon died. He didn't feel grief because he didn't know Shannon that well. He had talked to him, gambled with him, and drunk with him, but he didn't really know him. That bothered Tynan. He should feel something more at the death of one of his comrades, but he didn't. He felt tired and annoyed and suddenly hot.

Of course there was another consideration too. He was still in the field with men who still lived, and at the moment he had to try to keep them alive. The field was not the place to mourn the death of a fellow sailor.

It was something that he couldn't afford to do until he was back at Nha Be or on the ship. Then he would get drunk in honor of the dead.

Jones appeared and said, "Airlift will be here in about an hour. They've got a mission scheduled and will pick us up on their way back to Cu Chi."

Tynan took another look at the poncho-wrapped body and then stepped around a small, prickly bush to where Duke was eating a can of peaches.

"Want to check out the trees on the other side of the paddies before we go?" Tynan asked.

Duke looked up, squinted in the bright sunlight. He folded the top of the can back into the main cylinder and dropped it to the ground. "Be glad to."

"Take Carter and Boone with you. We'll cover you from here."

"You think there is going to be a problem?"

"I think Charlie probably didied out of there last night when all the shit started raining down on him. Just thought maybe we could get a body count for the cannon-cockers. Give them a thrill."

"Sure, Skipper." Duke stood up and put on his steel pot. He left his pack on the ground, next to the tree. There was no need to carry it on the sweep because he would be returning to the makeshift camp.

Duke moved to where Boone was leaning against a palm tree, his eyes closed. He slapped Boone on the shoulder and, when he saw him stir, said, "Get your weapon. We're going to check out the artillery."

He collected Carter, and the three of them left the trees, wading through the center of the rice paddies hoping to avoid any booby traps that Charlie might have scattered along the tops of the dikes. They walked in the ankle-deep brown water, stepping on the plants because that kept their feet from sinking deeply in the mud.

Cautiously they entered the trees, circling the machine-gun emplacement. The trees around them had been shredded by the shrapnel of the 105 shells. The bark was peeled back in places and branches hung down. The green leaves had been stripped from some of them, and Duke knew that in a day or so the trees would take on the dull gray look of those killed by artillery or by overhead bombing.

The ground was blackened by the fires started by the Willy Pete, or it was dark brown where it had been overturned by the mushrooming of the artillery. There were broken bits of tree and bush lying around, and scattered among the remains of the vegetation was a little raw meat. Bits of flesh that now looked rusty and out of place. Except for a single intact lung that seemed to have been set on a rotting log with the loving care of a pathologist.

Carter took one look at the lung and turned his head as if he were going to throw up, but he didn't. Instead, he turned slowly so that he could take a longer, better look at it and then stepped forward and placekicked the lung into the palm trees nearby.

"Why the fuck did you do that?" asked Duke quietly.

Carter shook his head. "Seemed like the thing to do."

Duke took a final look around, but there were no weapons other than the broken bits of the machine gun. He found one shattered stock from an AK-47. But there were no bodies or blood trails. It looked as if the machine gun had taken a direct hit, and that meant that the gunner and his assistant were probably killed; the lung proved that someone had died. Duke shrugged and waved the men out of the trees.

It was longer than an hour before the helicopters arrived. Tynan threw smoke and the lead aircraft landed, putting his nose in the middle of the billowing cloud of green. Tynan and Duke tossed the body into the cargo compartment, and Boone helped Turner into the aircraft. In seconds everyone was loaded and the choppers took off, climbing out toward the north and the Saigon River before banking back to the east and Cu Chi. The flight was short. They didn't land along the main runway at Cu Chi, but shot the approach to a small pad in front of the 12th Evac Hospital. Just as the skids touched the ground, three men wearing white burst through the doors of the hospital. One of them pushed a gurney as another tried to steer it. The third carried an OD—olive drab—knapsack with a large red cross on it.

They slid to a halt near the helicopter and looked disappointed when Turner, the lopsided bandage around his calf flapping, hopped down. The man with the knapsack helped Turner onto the gurney, and as they rushed back into the hospital the helicopter lifted off, toured the traffic pattern, and landed near the perimeter where graves registration was hidden.

Tynan and Duke shoved the body toward the door as a tall, thin man with short and very light blond hair left the small gray building. He had a sunken chest and thin arms and looked like the Army had been right in assigning him to graves registration. Tynan had never seen a man who looked more at home in his job.

He grabbed at the poncho and halted the body partway out of the chopper. He leaned in and shouted, "ID tags with the stiff?"

Tynan nodded and yelled, "You notify the Navy at Nha Be?"

"Right." He jerked on the poncho, let the body fall to the PSP that made up the pad, and then rolled it to the side, out of the way. Lying on the ground there, wrapped in poncho liners or zipped into OD body bags, were another three soldiers. There was a hole in one of the bags, and Tynan could see a blood-stained hand protruding from it.

They flew around the traffic pattern again and landed on a pad near the runway. Across a red dirt road was a company area, and as the engine of the Huey wound down, the pilot took off his helmet and yelled back at them, "You guys can wait in operations if you want. Or in the mess hall."

Tynan hopped out and reached back, grabbing his pack. With the CAR-15 in his left hand, he pointed at a heavily sandbagged structure just across the road. "That operations?" he asked.

"Yeah," said the pilot.

"Okay," said Tynan. He turned to Duke and said, "Why don't you have the boys wait in the mess hall. I'll go down and see what I can learn. I'll meet you in the mess hall in fifteen or twenty minutes."

Duke looked at the other men sitting in the helicopter and then leaned close to Tynan. "You okay, Skipper?"

"I'm fine," said Tynan. "Meet you in a little while."

Tynan hoisted his pack up so that it was dangling from his right shoulder. He crossed the road and stopped at the entrance to the operations bunker. A narrow stairway led down. Tynan dropped his gear on the sidewalk made from two-by-twelves and descended. He opened the rough wooden door and saw a wooden counter in front of him. Behind it was a board containing the names of the flight crews and their aircraft assignments. A spec four was busily writing information in black grease pencil on the board.

He turned and waved Tynan in. "Close the fucking door," he ordered. "All the fucking cold air is going to fucking get out of here, and then it will be fucking hotter than a bitch in heat in here."

Tynan did as he was told. He noticed that there was an area to his right that contained several tables and maps and figured that the pilots used it for flight planning. He moved in that direction and then stopped, wondering just what in the hell he was doing down there.

The spec four finished what he had been doing and said, "Can I help you?"

"The operations officer around?"

"Nope. He's flying. So's the exec. Everybody's flyin' today. Anything I can do for you?" The man held up his hand and added, "And before you ask, the CO went up to battalion a little while ago, so he's not around either."

Tynan looked at the spec four. He was a kid, probably not much more than eighteen. He was wearing standard-issue jungle fatigues that looked freshly laundered, but then it was cool in the bunker and not like the humid air outside. He had the beginnings of a mustache on his upper lip and short blond hair that hadn't been combed recently. He was a small kid who looked like he had just escaped from high school.

Tynan stared at him for a moment. "No. I don't think so."

"Suit yourself." The kid sat down, nearly disappearing behind the counter. To his left was a rack of radios, each with tiny lights glowing. Tynan could hear the radio messages being passed back and forth by the flight crews.

Tynan started back up the stairs, figuring that he would find Duke and talk to him. For some reason, Tynan felt lost. He didn't know what he wanted to do. He was confused by all that had happened, from Walker refusing to alert the Army that the VC might want to overrun a fire-support base to the ambush they had blundered into the night before.

He reached the top of the stairs and stopped to pick up his gear when he saw Duke approaching.

"What's the word, Skipper?"

Tynan started to shrug and then stopped. "We hit the field again in a couple of hours."

"Really?" asked Duke. "You don't think we've got enough?"

"Come on, Paul, all we got is shit. We saw some guys who looked like they've been slinging packs down the Ho Chi Minh Trail and we saw some guys who didn't look like they were having a good time farming, but we didn't get shit."

"Okay," said Duke. He looked at the rubberized green sandbags that lined the wall of the operations bunker. They formed a wall that was about waist high. He leaped up on them so that he was seated facing Tynan.

"That all you want to say?"

Duke shrugged. "You're the skipper," he said. "Hell, I didn't like pulling out of the field this morning, but who am I to comment? Besides, what the hell is a bunch of sailors doing screwing around this far from the water?"

"Yeah," said Tynan. "I've been trying to figure that out myself. Seems to me, though, that we've only half finished the job. Found evidence that the VC are in the Hobo Woods, but that's no surprise to anyone.

Maybe we should just go back out, look around a little, and then mosey on into the fire-support base.''

''When do we do this?''

''Well, I figured that we could grab some real food here first and get back into the field this afternoon. I could talk to somebody and get us a ride out.''

Duke jumped down from the sandbags. ''I'll tell the boys. They thought we were going to get a trip to the ship or maybe back to Nha Be.''

''I hope this doesn't disappoint them too much.''

Duke wiped a hand across his face. He looked at the sweat and then rubbed his palm against the front of his fatigue jacket. ''I think they might like the opportunity to get even with Charlie,'' he said.

''We did that last night,'' replied Tynan.

''Yes, sir. Except it was the cannon-cockers who got even for us. I think they want a chance to do something on their own. Something where they can see some results right away.''

''All right,'' the lieutenant said. ''You tell the boys, and I'll find someone around here to get us a ride into the field.''

Duke headed for the mess hall while Tynan strolled the company area. He heard the sound of a radio or a TV coming from a hootch that had sandbags around the walls and a tin roof over it. There were a dozen wires strung among the hootches and a series of bunkers dug to one side. He opened the door and stepped into a miniature dayroom. Two men in flight suits sat in dilapidated lawn chairs, staring at a small black-and-white TV that sat on a bar constructed from the odds and ends of scrap lumber.

He turned and looked at the screen. There was some kind of local weather program going that looked almost like a parody of all the weather shows on local stations in the World. A map of Vietnam hung behind a girl in an extremely short dress. A large cold front was drawn on the map and there was a lot of numbers, the highs and lows for the day. When the girl turned to point at something on the map, a bucket of water was thrown at her, soaking her clothes so that they molded themselves to her body. It was quite a good body, Tynan could see.

Then, without thinking, he said, "Hey, I know that girl."

One of the men looked at him with a bored expression on his face and said, "You know Bobbi?"

Tynan stared at the TV. Bobbi was wearing stockings and black panties. That was suddenly obvious from the way she bent over to try to wring the water from her long hair. Tynan smiled as he watched her, thinking as he had on the night he had danced with her on the roof of the Oriental that she had the best-looking legs he had ever seen. He smiled as he thought about how he had seen just how good they were.

To the men in the hootch, he said, simply, "Yeah, I know Bobbi."

"Well, quick," said one of the men, "tell mc how to meet her. I think I love her."

"Only because she has round eyes," said the other, staring at the TV screen.

"Who the fuck was looking at her eyes?"

"Either of you know where I can find the CO?" said Tynan, hoping that neither of them ever got to meet Bobbi.

"He's probably in his hootch if he's not down in operations."

"And where is his hootch?"

"Out the door, straight down the walk. It's the last one before you step into the street. Right near the latrine. Seems to be the appropriate place for it."

Tynan said, "Thanks," and left. He stopped just outside the door and wondered if maybe he shouldn't just find a way to fly back to Saigon. Bobbi had said that she would like to see him again, and Tynan desperately wanted to see her. They had spent a quiet evening on the roof dancing and then had left together. What followed had not been quiet.

Instead of that, he made his way to the CO's hootch, found that the man was in, and requested that his men be airlifted back into the field, near Trung Lap. The CO, who was sitting in his air-conditioned hootch, drinking a beer and writing a letter, just grunted once and then added, "When we go out this afternoon, you can get on the last two ships. They can drop you off before we hit the PZ for the infantry."

Tynan thanked him and left, heading for the mess hall so that he could brief his men. He stopped once, near the hootch where he had seen Bobbi on the TV but now heard Captain Kirk announce that space was the final frontier.

"You haven't been to the Hobo Woods," Tynan told him.

Tynan watched the ground seem to leap toward them as the helicopter swooped out of the sky, dropping away from the formation as if it had been hit by ground fire and lost the ability to fly. There was a single green smoke grenade burning on the ground in front of them, dropped by the gunship that led them to the LZ. As the helicopter flared Tynan lost sight of the smoke, and then they were down, among the low trees and tall bushes and razorlike elephant grass that grew in the Hobo Woods.

Tynan and his men jumped from the helicopters, and as soon as they were out, the choppers pulled pitch, climbing into the sky and racing after the flight they had just left. Without a word, Tynan's men headed for the nearest of the tree lines so that they could get oriented and begin a new search for the VC.

They entered the trees and turned south, away from the Saigon River, heading more or less in the direction of Trung Lap. They avoided a couple of small hamlets that crouched in stands of palm and coconut trees. They crossed a small stream that was clear and cool and full of leeches. They halted in the trees and passed a can of insect repellent around, spraying the leeches. For some reason the nasty creatures hated the sting of the repellent and released the victim. Jones, who couldn't look at the bloodsuckers hanging on his own body, stamped on them as they dropped to the ground, covering his boot with blood.

They marched through the afternoon as the hanging sun fell toward the horizon and the heat of the day built to its peak. Tynan felt tired and then dizzy and finally both. He realized that even the slow pace they were following was becoming too much in the humidity and heat. He finally called a halt, letting the men slip to the ground where they stood. He circled them carefully, making sure that a tiny perimeter was established and that no one let down his guard. Each man took a deep swallow from one of his canteens. Jones poured half of the water on an OD hand towel he had wrapped around his neck and then wiped away the sweat. He took off his steel pot and set it on the ground beside him. He got a Hershey bar out of one of his pockets and unwrapped it. He took one look at the gooey mess and then carefully folded the paper and buried it.

Fifteen minutes later Tynan was on his feet, ready to move out. He tapped Jones on the shoulder and said quietly, "Give the radio back to Carter and take the point."

"Sure, Skipper. Direction of travel?"

"Try one-six-zero until we hit the road. Looks abandoned according to the map, but halt short of it. We'll take a look then."

Jones got out his own map and consulted it, looking for landmarks that would make staying on course easier. Then he sighted through his compass, snapped it shut, and said, "Whenever."

Just as Tynan was going to rise, they heard a burst of sound, voices, coming from the trees in front of them. Tynan slipped quietly to a prone position, easing his CAR-15 forward and thumbing off the safety.

Jones looked at the older man, raised his eyebrows in question, and then seemed to sink downward as he let his body relax while he waited to find out what was happening.

The voice came again. A sharp voice that had an edge to it. There was a muted response, and through the trees Tynan could see a man in a green uniform. Behind him were four others, and in front was a single man in black pajamas. Each carried a weapon of Soviet design.

Tynan wanted to warn the others to stay quiet but could not move without giving them away. As he watched, more NVA and VC appeared. Three of them struggled with a mortar and its base plate. A couple of others carried RPG-7s. Tynan counted thirty-two men before he quit. Suddenly he knew that the attack on Crockett would be that night, and that he was very close to one of the staging points.

Silently they fell back, putting some distance between them and the enemy unit that had appeared in front of them. Tynan was surprised that the VC and NVA could move so many men through the Hobo Woods without making any noise. It was almost as if they had just sprung from the ground.

Tynan and his men swept onward. Tynan glanced at the sun that was now high overhead, beating down on them relentlessly, sapping their strength as they fought their way through the undergrowth. He wanted to stop frequently to rest and to drink from his canteen, but he knew that he was letting the sun get to him. He forced himself and the patrol forward, ignoring the bruising heat of the afternoon.

They wormed their way through one tree line, across open ground covered only by ankle-hugging grass, and entered another stand of trees. From somewhere beyond they heard voices speaking Vietnamese and heard hammering, as if the Vietnamese were building something. Tynan waved his men to the ground and crawled forward slowly.

He reached the edge of the trees and saw a small village in front of him. There were fifteen or twenty mud hootches. Three of them had metal roofs reflecting the bright sun. The others had thatch. A couple of water-buffalo pens stood at the edge of the ville. A mud fence along a small, shallow canal bordered the western side. Women, both young and old, most with teeth stained black by the betel nuts they chewed, were squatting near fires and cooking pots. Several young men were hammering on long, thin wooden boxes.

"Those what I think they are?" asked Duke.

Tynan took a closer look. They didn't have the funny shape caused by the widening where the shoulders were to be, but the boxes were obviously coffins.

"Yeah, I think so," whispered Tynan.

"I count forty-two finished," said Duke.

Tynan nodded and pointed toward the canal and fence on their right. "Looks like they have ladders there."

"Ladders for what?"

"To throw over the wire as they storm the base," responded Tynan.

"Funny they're working out in the open like that," said Duke.

Tynan was going to agree until he looked at the location of the ville. Like most of the others they had seen, it was set back in a large grove of trees, the palm branches extending outward, shielding the village from the sky. Tynan was sure that the original reason for building the hamlets in groves of tall trees was for the shade and the protection from the monsoon rains. Now they kept the prying eyes of the American pilots from seeing them.

Tynan watched as a group of men stood and walked back to one of the hootches. They hesitated at the entrance and then disappeared inside. A couple of minutes later, they reappeared, carrying some more of the light-colored lumber. Tynan studied them carefully. There was something about them that he didn't quite understand. It seemed that they had changed clothes while in the hootch. That bothered Tynan for some reason that he couldn't quite put his finger on.

Finally Duke asked, "You seen enough?"

"Yeah. This pretty well confirms it. Charlie wouldn't be building coffins if he didn't expect to take some casualties. This is the last thing he does before the attack. I think we'd better get to Crockett as quickly as we can."

"Let's just radio the Army and get the fuck out of here."

"I'm not sure that's such a swell idea," said Tynan, shaking his head. "We don't want to tip our hand." There were a dozen other things that Tynan could have said, but he didn't think it was the time or the place to get into a discussion of military tactics. He knew that the Army wanted the VC and the NVA to come out and fight because the Army knew that in a stand-up fight against the Vietnamese guerrillas, American soldiers could not be beaten.

"So what do we do?"

"We slip out of here as quietly as possible and head direct to Crockett."

Duke nodded and began to creep backward slowly, keeping his eyes fastened on the men and women in the ville. Overhead, he heard the sound of a chopper. The people looked up, but none of them moved, as if they believed that making any move would betray their presence to the pilots.

When Tynan and Duke rejoincd the main body of the patrol, they began to slip through the woods, hurrying in the direction of Fire-Support Base Crockett. They wanted to avoid open areas where the VC might have planted booby traps for landing helicopters or left snipers. They wanted to stay to the cover that was available in the trees, but they also wanted to make time.

They had entered a small section of woods and had spread out through it. They moved slowly, cautiously, slipping from one point to the next, listening for the enemy. Overhead there were dozens of helicopters, but none of them seemed interested in what was happening on the ground.

As the trees thinned, Tynan halted his men. He thought they could rest a moment. He leaned against a palm. To the right he heard a noise and turned toward it. He rolled to his belly and crawled forward. In front of him he saw another VC platoon setting up. There were a couple of men working around a mortar and base plate. Suddenly two more appeared, and then two more. In a couple of minutes, the clearing seemed to be swarming with VC and NVA. Tynan shook his head as if he couldn't believe it. The VC kept appearing.

6

The sun had fallen below the horizon, and it was obvious that the VC and NVA weren't going to move very soon. They had dropped their packs and stacked their rifles. They had scraped together dry wood and started a couple of nearly smokeless cooking fires. They filtered from the campsite, farther into the trees, one of them stopping not more than six feet from Tynan, but the enemy was more concerned with his dinner of rice cakes and fishheads and didn't see the SEAL lying concealed in the bushes.

Tynan had barely breathed for the last hour. He had watched as the VC dipped his hand into the small bag of rice and then used his tongue to lick his palm clean. He had seen the man eat the fishheads and heard him burp twice. When he finished eating, the enemy used a knife to scrape at the ground to bury the remains of his meal. Then, carefully, he spread dried leaves and dead vegetation over the hole so that it was nearly invisible.

Tynan glanced to the right and could see Jones still crouched by the PRC-25. He had frozen the moment that the VC had appeared at the edge of the trees. The last movement Jones had made was to make sure that the radio was turned off.

Moving only his eyes, Tynan looked to the right and, staring into the darkening landscape, thought that he could see Carter lying on his side, his rifle cradled in his arms. Not one of his men had so much as flinched since the VC had moved in.

As the last of the sunlight faded away, Tynan saw the VC put out their fires. Using the leaves of the palms and the jungle plants, they could dissipate the smoke so that it couldn't be seen from above, but they could do nothing with the flames. The light was too easy to spot from too many directions at night. And as the fires died so did the talking. There were only whispered instructions.

Tynan watched as they assembled their mortar tube and base plate and stacked the ammunition for it. When they did that, Tynan knew that they wouldn't be moving, even after the attack started, but by lobbing mortars at the American fire-support base they could draw return artillery fire away from the assault troops. Tynan didn't want to be around as the 105mm shells began exploding among the trees.

An hour after it was totally dark, and before the moon began to rise, some of the enemy soldiers began to gather their equipment. They shouldered their rifles and started forming up in the southwest corner of the camp. When they were ready, they filtered out, disappearing into the night.

Tynan made another quick count and discovered that only seven VC remained behind. He slowly moved his hand upward along his web gear until he touched his Randall combat knife. The blade was not shiny like most knives, but dulled so that it would not reflect light. The edges were razor sharp and could cut through the toughest leather with little effort.

Slowly, knife held at the ready, Tynan moved one hand, setting it carefully among the fallen leaves and dry twigs from the trees. He put his weight on it cautiously and then moved his foot. In minutes he had a rhythm going that allowed him to move silently through the woods until he was near one of his own soldiers.

Jones saw him seem to loom out of the darkness. Tynan grinned, showed the man his knife, and then pointed at the enemy. Jones nodded his understanding and moved off to alert Boone. Tynan reversed his course and went to let Carter know that they were going to attack the Viet Cong mortar emplacement with their knives.

Once he had done that, Tynan turned and began working his way through the trees toward the VC soldiers. There was one nearly in front of him, sitting with his back to a log, his head bowed as if he were praying or sleeping.

Out of the corner of his eye, Tynan could see another of his men creeping forward, using the little brush available for cover. He held his knife in his right hand, the point thrust out toward the enemy.

Tynan glanced away from his victim, afraid that he might somehow communicate his intent if he stared at the man's back. He carefully rocked back on his feet so that he was ready to spring. Then from overhead came the popping of a recon chopper, and as the noise enveloped the area and the VC looked upward, Tynan leaped.

His left hand lifted the chin of the VC as he slashed at the throat with the knife in his right. He cut deeply, severing the arteries and veins. Blood splashed down the front of the man and spurted out onto the ground. As Tynan plunged his knife into the man's chest just below the breastbone, the man spasmed and kicked his feet, his heels drumming on the soft earth. Tynan twisted the knife blade so that it penetrated the heart and pierced a lung. The man went rigid, as if trying to hold on to life by sheer force of muscle and will, and then collapsed, a rattling in his throat as the last of the air burped from him.

Another VC loomed out of the dark, staring at the dead man as if he didn't understand what had happened. Tynan leaped across the log and the dead man, grabbing the living enemy. He forced his left hand over the VC's mouth and nose and drove his knife into the man's ribs. The enemy staggered back, his fingers clawing at the holster he wore on one hip. Tynan punched at him, his hand hitting the enemy in the neck. There was a startled gasp as the soldier fell to his knees, both hands digging at his throat. Tynan kicked upward, the heel of his boot snapping the man's head back, breaking his neck as he fell over.

Jones had killed one man easily, using his knife and nearly severing the enemy's head. A second man came at him, but Jones turned to meet the threat, kicked once, and dropped the VC. He leaped to his chest, both of his knees driving into the soldier's rib cage as he shoved his knife into the soft spot at the base of the throat.

Near Jones, Sterne knifed a VC, first with a blow to the lower back to scramble the kidney, and then forcing the blade upward so that it would pierce the heart. He let the VC sink to the ground.

Tynan turned and saw Boone standing over the body of a dead soldier. Boone then dropped to one knee, stared into the darkness, and looked at Tynan. He held a thumb up to tell the skipper that he was all right.

Carter had failed to find a target. He moved out of the trees as quietly as the rest, but the enemy soldiers were all out of sight. He made his way to the mortar tube, capturing it before the enemy could mount a counterattack.

Tynan caught Carter's eye and pointed at the trees on the other side of the VC camp. Carter nodded, slipped his knife into the sheath, and unslung his M-16. He moved forward slowly, watching the ground and bushes around him. He found no one there and saw no signs of any kind of rear guard left by the majority of the enemy as they had departed.

Just as Tynan stepped close to Duke, who was now kneeling next to the mortar tube trying to figure out how to destroy it without making any noise, there was a series of pops.

"Incoming," shouted Boone as he dropped to the ground.

Tynan hesitated, looking for the flash in the trees, but saw nothing. Then, nearly a minute later, they heard the explosions as they drifted on the evening air.

"That's the VC starting the assault," said Tynan.

"We could lob some mortars at them," said Duke.

"Too risky. We don't know where the LPs are. Crockett's got to have some people in LPs. We might hit them by accident."

"Sounds like we're too late," said Duke. "LPs should have been pulled in by now."

Tynan turned and looked toward the sound of the explosions. He could see nothing. "We can still hit the VC from the rear," he said. "Maybe find one of their reserve units and cause a little trouble."

"What about the tube?" asked Duke.

"Pack it with mud and leave it. Booby-trap it if you can think of something." He turned and called, "Jones, you want to take the point. Same compass heading."

Jones stepped close and began to take out his map.

Tynan stopped him. "Just follow the compass course and the sound of the firing. We'll get there.

But watch your step—the closer we get the more of the enemy who will be around.''

As Jones headed off, Tynan said, "Paul, I want you to bring up the rear. We've got to be careful on this one. Don't let anyone get behind us, and if you get into trouble, use your rifle. A little extra rifle fire probably won't be noticed with all the other shooting going on out here.''

While Duke finished packing the mortar tube with mud and then tried to booby-trap it so that the VC would blow themselves up, the patrol formed and began to move. Tynan stayed close to the front and let the others, Carter, Sterne, and Boone, string out behind him.

He didn't take time to think about the men he had just killed. They had been enemy soldiers, and although they had been humans, they would have killed him, given the chance. Maybe later, after he got out of the trees and out of the heat and humidity, he would take time to think about it. But now all he could do was move forward, being careful where he placed his feet so that he didn't make noise and didn't trip a booby trap, and watch Jones, who was hurrying to the fire-support base.

Jones stopped suddenly, waving a hand behind him, telling Tynan to take cover. In the distance he could hear the rattle of small arms as the VC attempted to take the fire-support base. He could hear the firing of the 105s as the artillerymen tried to break up the enemy assault forces. There were explosions in the trees far away as the artillery shells landed, and overhead he could hear but not see helicopters searching for enemy troop concentrations.

Tynan waited for a few moments and then saw Jones coming back. He reached out so that Jones would see him, and when the man approached, Tynan whispered, "What is it?"

"Platoon-size force in front of us."

"Doing what?"

"Milling around and playing with their weapons. I think they're waiting for their turn to kill the running dogs and imperialist swine."

"How far?"

"I was about twelve, fifteen meters from them when I spotted them. Trees thin out quite a bit and there was a little clearing. They were in it."

"All right," said Tynan. "Wait here." He crawled back and found Carter, who now had the M-79. He pulled Sterne in close and went after Boone. Duke joined them a couple of moments later.

"Here's the plan," whispered Tynan. "We'll work our way to the edge of the trees. Carter, you pump out as many rounds with the M-79 as you can. The rest of us will throw grenades. That should scatter the VC."

"If they charge us?" asked Duke.

"We cut them down with rifle fire."

"And then?" asked Sterne.

"We fall back to here if we need to. If not, we'll continue our advance toward Crockett. Any other questions?" He waited a moment and then said, "Your signal to throw the grenades is the sound of Carter's M-79."

They moved forward to the edge of the trees. Each of them took a grenade, pulled the pin, and waited for the pop of Carter's weapon. When it came, they each threw their grenades as far as they could and then crouched behind the available cover of the palm and coconut trees around them.

There was a single crash in the center of the Vietnamese when the grenade from the M-79 exploded in a miniature fountain of sparks and invisible shrapnel. Several of them screamed, some in pain and some in terror. Two or three fell to the ground and began to indiscriminately spray the surrounding trees with green-and-white tracers from their AK-47s.

Then, suddenly, there was a series of explosions in the clearing from the hand grenades. The VC tried to flee in all directions, leaving their dead and wounded in the field. A dozen of them rushed the tree line where Tynan and his men crouched. Two of them came running straight at Tynan, and he stood to meet the threat, his CAR-15 out in front of him. One of the VC, surprised by the sudden appearance of a man where there should have been none, changed his course slightly, raising his hands as if he wanted to grab Tynan. Tynan ducked under the outstretched arms like a quarterback shedding a linebacker. He swung the butt of his weapon to the rear, smashing the enemy soldier in the small of the back, driving him to the ground.

The second Viet Cong was suddenly in front of him, and Tynan pulled the trigger of his weapon. Three rounds slammed into the VC's stomach and chest, throwing him back into the clearing, where his blood spurted from his body as his heart raced. He started to sit up and then collapsed, dead.

Tynan spun, kicked at the first VC, missed, and then fired a single shot that penetrated the back of the enemy's helmet. The round blew out the face of the soldier, blinding him, breaking his jaw, and carrying away part of his skull, but he never knew it. He was dead before he had fallen to the ground.

There was sporadic firing around Tynan. He saw a couple of ruby tracers from American weapons dance into the night and heard a return shot from an AK-47 that was quickly silenced. The lieutenant stared into the darkness, trying to see what was happening in the clearing, but there was no movement there now.

Duke stepped close and said, "And now?"

"We bug out. Head to the east and try to find a way into the fire-support base."

Duke turned and yelled, "Let's go!"

Tynan caught Jones and said, "Compass course of zero-nine-zero for about a klick."

"Yes, sir," said Jones as he disappeared down the long axis of the tree line, staying to the cover available there. He moved quickly but deliberately, trying to get out of the general area as fast as possible.

They had only gone a couple of hundred meters when they heard the pop of mortars nearby. The men fell to the ground as the rounds whistled overhead, exploding near the place where they had ambushed the VC platoon.

Tynan crawled to Jones, hit him on the foot to get his attention, and pointed to the east. Jones nodded his understanding and began to crawl in that direction.

Again Duke appeared and said, "We got out of there just in time."

"Yeah."

They continued on, the moon now up and casting a bright light over the landscape. They could see the tree lines in front and on the sides as black shapes with blacker shadows. Overhead there was the popping of parachute flares fired by the artillery of the fire-support bases, giving the Americans at Crockett the light they needed to see the enemy sappers.

They came to the end of the trees, to a large open area that was about five hundred meters from the outer perimeter wire of Crockett. They could hear the outgoing rifle and machine-gun fire as it ripped through the night. From the bunker line, they could see the flashes of the muzzles like the flashbulbs of a thousand cameras. Ruby tracers filled the night, red streaks of fire stabbing out toward the enemy, trying to hold them in the distance.

Directly in front of them, Tynan could see nearly a full company of NVA regulars. These were hardcore troops. Tynan could tell because, in the flickering yellowish light of the parachute flares, he could see they were wearing khaki uniforms. They were formed into three ranks, crouching, waiting for their turn to sweep forward to Crockett.

To the right of the formation there was a single bush. A man came from underneath it. A moment later there was a second man, and then a third. They took places at the side of the enemy company, facing forward, their weapons held at the ready.

Tynan watched them for a minute as they watched the battle raging in front of them. Mortars hidden in the trees somewhere farther to the east popped and flashed in response to the crashing of the 105s that the Americans were using. Tynan glanced to his right, saw Boone, and crawled to him, taking the handset of the radio.

"Cu Chi Arty," he whispered. "I have a fire mission."

"This is Cu Chi Arty," replied an angry voice. "We have no artillery available."

Tynan looked at the handset in disbelief and then realized that all the artillery in the vicinity would be on call to support Crockett. Each of the fire-support bases had interlocking fields of fire with the others in the area, and when one was attacked, the others stood by to lend support.

Boone switched off the radio and asked, "We going to take these guys?"

"Sure," whispered Tynan. He wished that they had opted to bring a couple of claymore mines. Set properly, the 750 ball bearings fired by the C-4 charge could almost wipe out the enemy company in front of him. But they weighed too much to be carried for any distance by such a small patrol as the one that Tynan was leading. They had too much other equipment that they had to have.

Tynan decided to split his force into two-man groups and spread them through the trees. Carter, who had the M-79, would be in the center group and once the firing started would pump grenades through his weapon unless there was an assault on the trees by the VC. Then he would use the canister rounds, which were like giant shotgun shells.

Quietly the Americans moved into position. Tynan set his grenades on the ground in front of him so that he could grab them quickly. Next to them he set the handheld parachute flares that he could launch if he needed them.

Finally he set a couple of magazines for his CAR-15 next to the grenades so that he could switch them quickly if he had to. The bandolier that he wore held the rest, but it could be difficult to remove the magazines in the middle of a firefight.

Tynan waited a couple of seconds, letting the other members of his team get ready. In front of him two or three of the NVA walked among the troops, shouting at them in Vietnamese, as if telling them that a great victory would soon be theirs. Tynan had been in Vietnam long enough to understand some of the language, and he knew from reports he had read that political officers often told the VC and NVA before the battle that this was the last American outpost and when it was destroyed the war would end. Good propaganda, but clearly not true with American aircraft filling the skies.

He picked up a grenade, pulled the pin, and waited, the safety lever held firmly in place. He wasn't sure what he was waiting for. Finally he tossed the grenade, trying to arc it over the troops so that it would land in front of them. He picked up a second grenade and threw it, and then a third and fourth.

The first grenade exploded by itself. There was a shout of alarm from the VC and a single burst of machine-gun fire directed into the trees away from Tynan and his men. Then a second grenade detonated, and a third and fourth, until it seemed that American artillery was raining into the clearing where the VC waited.

For an instant the enemy held their positions, confused by the sudden explosions. There was screaming from the wounded and the dying and firing by men who didn't have a target but who had to shoot at something.

Then, almost as if someone had given a command, those in the company who survived turned and ran for the trees behind them. It was an uncoordinated rush with no one shooting or trying to defend themselves.

There was a boom as Carter fired the first of his canister rounds, and a dozen of the VC collapsed as the pellets penetrated the line. One M-16 opened fire, raking the VC. It was quickly joined by another and another, until all of Tynan's men were firing into the ranks of the enemy as fast as they could pull the trigger and change magazines.

The attack faltered and halted as the VC stopped, confused by the shooting coming from the trees. They turned, running right and left, some of them throwing away their weapons. Others stumbled over the wounded and fell. One or two fired into the trees, but their muzzle flashes gave them away and Tynan's men returned the fire with a deadly accuracy that quickly silenced them.

The firing around them grew to an almost continuous roar and then tapered as the number of targets decreased. Tynan grabbed one of his flares and jammed the butt into his thigh so that the firing pin hit the propellant. There was a sudden burst of light overhead as the flare went off.

A VC, surprised, turned his weapon skyward, trying to shoot down the flare. He missed, but Tynan cut him down with a burst in the back.

As the flare fell to the ground and sputtered and died, the firing tapered off until it was only a couple of well-spaced shots. From the fire-support base, there was still a fusillade, but the company that had been waiting to reinforce the attackers was either dead or scattered.

"Let's fall back," shouted Tynan as he withdrew from the front of the tree line.

The others in the patrol gathered near him, each taking a position where he could cover a small portion of the tiny perimeter. Tynan took out the small book of radio call signs that he carried. He searched through it until he found the radio frequency used by the troops at Fire-Support Base Crockett, along with the call sign.

He grabbed the handset from the radio and turned it on. When he heard the carrier wave, he squeezed the mike button and said quietly, "Black Label Six, this is Black Baron Six."

There was a pause and a crackle of static and then: "Go, Black Baron Six."

"We're on the ground outside the perimeter."

"Outside the perimeter?"

"Roger. We need to get inside."

"Ah, wait one, Black Baron Six."

Tynan didn't say a word. He clutched the handset in a death grip and watched the parachute flares over the fire-support base drift toward the ground and listened to the sound of the artillery firing. Overhead were a dozen helicopters, searching for the enemy, periodically dropping out of the sky to light up the ground with rocket fire and bursts from their miniguns that looked like red rays from space weapons.

"Black Baron Six. Say intentions."

"I say again," repeated Tynan, "we need to get inside."

"Wait one."

There was a momentary pause, and then the radio crackled again. "Do you have flares?"

"Roger." Tynan was getting angry.

"Approach from the November side of the Foxtrot Tango Bravo. When three-zero-zero meters, fire a Gulf flare."

Tynan rolled his eyes but understood the message. He was to approach the fire-support base from the north and, when he was about three hundred meters away, fire a green flare. That would identify his location for the defenders in the camp. He gave the handset back to Boone and said, "Let's move out. Duke, take the point, and be careful."

Duke moved off to the east so that he was paralleling the perimeter of the fire-support base but was nearly half a klick from the wire. He crept forward cautiously, looking for signs of the VC, but found none. The firing in the distance had tapered off, as if the Viet Cong had momentarily broken off the attack.

Around them they could hear the pop of mortars being fired at the base and the crash of artillery in response. Flares still blossomed overhead, but the light was centered on the southern side of the camp, away from them. They could see shifting shapes of blacks and dark grays in the light, but saw no sign of enemy troops.

Duke halted when he came to a small dirt road that wound its way to the camp. He knew that most of the supplies for fire-support bases were flown in, but trucks and jeeps in convoys sometimes brought in replacements and additional equipment. There would be two heavily fortified and armored bunkers on either side of the gate.

Tynan approached, saw that it would be a long run in the open. And there was the problem of trigger-happy GIs in the bunkers firing at anyone who was running at them. Tynan held out his hand for the mike of the PRC-25.

Then he took out a red flare and armed it by putting the cap with the firing pin on the base of the tube. He keyed the mike and said, "Black Label, this is Black Baron Six. I'm firing the flare."

A moment later three arcs of green erupted around him. As Tynan had suspected, the VC were monitoring the radio frequencies from the fire base and had understood the message. That was why Tynan had not fired a green. His was the red one. Over the radio, he said, "Black Label, I fired the red. Be advised that the green marks the VC."

As he finished speaking the .50-caliber machine guns in the bunkers guarding the gate opened fire, their heavy red tracers lancing outward toward the base of the green flares. Seconds later HE from the 82mm mortars in the camp's defenses began to pepper the ground. It almost seemed that the .50s were marking the targets.

Tynan saw this and nearly yelled into the mike, "We're coming in. Right down the road." He tossed the mike at Boone and said, "Let's go."

He pointed at Duke, who took off running on the road. He was followed closely by Sterne and Carter. Jones was next, and then Boone leaped to his feet, running forward. Tynan hesitated a moment, waiting for the VC to open fire, but they didn't. He sprayed the trees near himself once, just in case, and then leaped up, running down the road, twenty meters behind his men.

They ran as fast as they could, ignoring the firing erupting around them. Tynan saw a couple of green tracers flash by but tried not to watch them. He believed that watching the tracers would draw them to him. He ran, his arms outstretched, holding his CAR-15 away from his body. He ran with the canteens on his hip pounding into him with each step and the bandolier that now held only a few spare magazines banging his side. He ran on, gulping at the hot, moist air, trying to catch his men and not see the increasing volume of enemy fire directed at him and the men of his patrol.

In front of him, one of the men grunted, stumbled, and fell heavily to the dirt road. Tynan ran to him, looked down, but could see no wound. "You okay?" he hissed through clenched teeth but got no response. He reached down, grabbed the man under his arm, and tried to lift.

Suddenly there was a second pair of hands helping him lift the wounded man. Tynan glanced at Sterne and said, "Let's go."

They ran then, each holding on to the wounded man under his arms, dragging him toward the base, the toes of his boots leaving ragged lines in the dirt of the road. As they approached the gate, the others had dropped off and were facing the way they had come, now firing their M-16s at the muzzle flashes of the enemy's weapons. Tynan let go of the wounded man's shoulder and spun, adding his CAR-15 to the firing. Behind him was the steady hammering of the .50-calibers and the yammering of the .30s as they tried to suppress the enemy.

The wire gate that was now behind them opened and a man yelled, "Get your asses in here."

Tynan grabbed the wounded man again, as did Sterne. Together they ran through the gate. The others followed, and as soon as they were inside, two American soldiers closed it. Tynan kept going until he could drop behind one of the bunkers. Then he turned over the wounded man and found out that Carter had died when a rifle bullet had penetrated the front of his helmet, killing him instantly.

Tynan then peeked up over the top of the bunker and saw the road where they had been standing erupt as VC mortar rounds began walking down it, moving relentlessly toward the gate. Countermortar rounds, fired by the camp's 82mm mortars, began crashing into the trees several hundred meters away.

Tynan looked up as an Army officer approached. He was wearing a flak jacket and a steel pot with a single silver oak leaf painted on the front. In the flickering light of the fires started by the enemy mortars and the dancing light of the flares swinging overhead, Tynan could see the man had a thick mustache and bushy dark eyebrows that seemed to meet on the bridge of his nose.

"Black Baron Six, I presume," said the Army colonel.

"Yes, sir," said Tynan. Then he grinned and said, "I would like to inform you that we have uncovered evidence that the VC plan a coordinated attack on your camp."

"Thanks."

7

The Army colonel detailed two of his men to take Carter's body to the area being used as a dispensary. He then looked at Tynan and said, ''Let's go to the command post. You can brief me about what's happening outside.''

''And my men?''

''Have them come along. We can decide where to put them in a couple of minutes.''

They ran, crouched over as the firing on the bunker line continued, along the road on the interior of the base, across an open area where helicopters would land, toward the sandbagged structures that surrounded the observation tower that was in the center of the camp. Near it were the six 105mm howitzers. As they ran by the commo bunker, obvious because of the radio antennas on it, the colonel pointed so that Tynan's men halted and entered. Tynan and the colonel continued until they were at the entrance of the command post.

They ran around the wall set four feet in front of the entrance so that it would absorb any shrapnel from mortars or grenades that landed near it. Most of the interior was wrapped in shadows, with only a single kerosene lantern burning. It was set on an old Army field table that was probably OD green, but in the bright, small pool of almost-white light created by the lantern, it was hard to tell. Two wooden folding chairs, also OD green, sat near it. There was a large-scale map on the table, and Tynan could see markings on it where the colonel had identified the threats against his base and written them down. A staff sergeant in field gear of a steel pot and flak jacket stood in one corner near a couple of radios set on another old table. Tiny lights glowed on the front panels. The sergeant held two mikes, one in each hand, and was giving firing coordinates into them as quickly as he could.

The colonel took off his steel pot once they were inside and set it on the table. He ran a hand through thick, wavy hair that was sweat damp. His face was streaked with dirt and grease. He moved to the table and pointed. "Show me where you were and tell me what you saw."

As best he could, Tynan pointed out the locations of the mortar platoon he had attacked and the infantry company he had shot up. He showed the colonel his path from the moment that he had landed north of Trung Lap as he searched for the enemy until he had run into the fire-support base. He explained about the coffins he had seen being built, and the ladders that the NVA had been constructing.

The colonel smiled at that and said, "Odds are that your average Charlie will never see one of those nice boxes. Officers get them. The grunts get dumped into unmarked graves and buried as quickly as possible. That is, if Charlie manages to drag the bodies away."

"What's the situation here, Colonel, ah . . ."

"Riordan. Frank Riordan," he said. "And right now the situation isn't all that bad. We've taken some casualties and sustained some damage, but I don't think they've made their real try yet. They're trying

to soften us up with mortars, rockets, and some snip-
ing.''

Tynan thought of all the firing he had heard as he
tried to penetrate the perimeter. He hadn't seen many
bodies, except for the ones his own men had created,
but he did think that a pitched battle had been fought,
was being fought.

"They're just testing us, looking for the weak
spots,'' said Riordan. "They haven't found much
yet.''

"Doesn't that let you know they're coming?'' asked
Tynan.

"Shit, Lieutenant, we've known that for weeks.
We just didn't know when. Hell, the sign was all over
the fucking place. Military-age men in the fields. No
mortar attacks for days. We didn't know they had their
whole force in the area, but we've been ready.''

Tynan collapsed into one of the chairs and heard it
groan under his weight and the weight of the equipment that he carried. For a moment he just stared at
a corner of the bunker where he could see a mound
of dirt that was leaking from one of the sandbags.
Then he began to laugh, not that anything was funny.
He stopped and said, "Two of my men dead, and you
knew the assault was coming.''

"What's that mean?''

Tynan rubbed a hand over his face. He could feel
the stubble from a couple days' growth of beard, and
he felt the grease from the camouflage paint he had
spread on.

"It means that a couple of days ago I found a package of documents that said the VC were going to make
a real effort to grab this base. I was told by my supe-
riors not to say anything until we had better proof of
an attack because they didn't want the Navy to look
bad in case it didn't happen. That's what the fuck I

was doing in the field. Looking for that proof when I ran right into the middle of the attack. And you knew about it all the time.''

''We knew the attack was coming,'' agreed Riordan. ''We didn't and don't know where they're rallying. I've had patrols out for days looking for them. We find forty, fifty men working the fields who weren't around last week, but nowhere near enough men to form a regiment for an assault.''

''Looks like we were a little late with the information, then,'' said Tynan.

''That mean you know the rally points?''

Tynan shook his head. ''It means nothing,'' he said angrily. He was thinking momentarily about his two dead men. Men he had worked with for weeks. He shook himself to rid himself of the thought because he didn't have the time to worry about it now. He would hoist a beer to their memory when the fight was over. But now he had to concentrate on the battle at hand and how to keep the rest of his men alive.

''Nothing,'' he repeated under his breath. Then, to Riordan, he said, ''A day late and a dollar short. Looks like we were no help at all.''

Riordan sat down opposite Tynan. ''I can't get you out of here until the morning. Nobody's going to bring a chopper in unless it's to evacuate critically wounded.'' Riordan laughed once—a single bark that contained no humor. ''Hell, tomorrow we won't be able to keep them out, but you'll have to wait until then.''

Tynan nodded and said, ''That's no problem. You got some place on the perimeter you want to put my boys? We're trained jungle fighters. The best there are.''

''Real bushmasters, huh?'' said Riordan with a grin. ''Well, we're not into jungle fighting tonight, but we could use the extra guns on the perimeter if you'd like a lesson on point defense.''

''Sounds fine.''

Riordan pointed at the staff sergeant. ''Meade, you want to take the lieutenant and his boys out to one of the bunkers on the north side and get them situated.''

''Yes, sir.'' Meade zipped up his flak jacket and picked up an M-14 that was standing in the corner near the radios. ''If you'll follow me, sir.''

Outside, Meade stopped as the 105s fired with a sound like that of all the jet engines in the world roaring at once. As the noise died away he asked, ''You done any point defense?''

'' 'Fraid not.''

''Well, sir, I can put you in with some of the experienced boys. Split you and your men into two groups and let you help out that way.''

''That's fine.'' Tynan instinctively ducked as the 105s fired again.

Meade laughed and said, ''You get used to it.''

At the commo bunker they picked up the rest of the SEALS. Then, crouching low, they dashed through the center of the fire-support base. Tynan was surprised that it was as small as it was and wondered if the VC and NVA stood a good chance of taking it. The base wasn't more than two hundred and fifty feet in diameter, and there were only two light companies manning the perimeter. A well-coordinated attack by the VC could overrun part of the bunker line before any kind of reinforcements or supporting fire could be brought to bear. Tynan was regretting his decision to fight his way into the camp.

They reached the bunker line, and Tynan was surprised. He had expected to have enclosed bunkers with firing slits, but these were only sandbagged foxholes. He could see that some of them contained automatic crew weapons, while others were merely firing positions for the grunts.

"Any particular way you want to disperse your men?" asked Meade.

"Yes," responded Tynan. "Duke, you take Jones and Boone and do what Sergeant Meade here tells you. Sterne, you stay with me."

"Yes, sir," answered Sterne.

Meade pointed at a man in the bunker who was wearing corporal's stripes instead of the insignia of a spec four. Meade said, "Clayton, you give the lieutenant here some guidance."

"Sure thing, Sarge."

As Meade turned to take Duke, Jones, and Boone to the next bunker, Clayton said, "We have two schools of thought. One is that we fight from behind the bunkers so that when Charlie throws in his satchel charges, he just blows up the bunker. The other is that we don't let Charlie close enough to throw in the satchel charges."

Sterne looked at Tynan and said, "This is fucking terrific."

Clayton grinned up at them. They could see that his face was covered with dirt. His eyes and teeth stood out in the dark background. "Charlie barely made it to the wire the first time. We didn't blow the claymores or the foogas. If he gets through the first strand of wire, we've got those surprises for him."

Before Clayton could say more, there was a single crash from the center of the fire-support base. Clayton reached up and jerked on the front of Tynan's fatigue jacket.

"Incoming," he screamed unnecessarily. "That's a fucking rocket."

Both Tynan and Sterne dived into the bunker as more rockets, joined by 60mm and 81mm mortars, began to rain down on the fire-support base. There were explosions near the center. Tynan turned and watched as the top blew off the observation tower. It stood upright for a moment and then slowly toppled to the ground like a drunken ox.

From the field near the trees and on the other side of the wire there were whistles and then bugles. A shout went up from nearly three hundred Vietnamese throats as they worked themselves into a frenzy for the charge across the open ground to the wire of the fire-support base.

Tynan looked to the front, squinting into the flickering eerie light from the flares as they burst overhead, trying to see the enemy, but heard only the shouting and the bugles and the whistles in the distance. Then, suddenly, the first strand of wire blew up in six different places as the sappers, unseen by the defenders, detonated the first of their bangalore torpedoes.

Firing broke out along the bunker line. Sporadic, single shots from the M-16s of the grunts and long, sustained bursts from the M-60 machine guns. Far to the right was the full-throated chug of a .50-caliber machine gun. A few Chicom grenades exploded in the wire, doing no damage.

Seconds later the second strand went up as the sappers crawled closer, blowing paths through the wire for the assault troops. Then, rising out of the rice paddies near the tree lines, the attacking troops stood, shouting and screaming as they began a mad rush across the open ground, firing their weapons as they ran.

"Here they come," shouted Clayton, the excitement in his voice unmistakable.

Tynan was firing slowly, aiming his weapon and picking his targets as they ran at him. Few of them dropped out of the formation as it reached the first strand of wire and ran through it. At that moment the last of the concertina exploded. The sappers, having finished that part of the job, waited for the attacking infantry to catch them.

The enemy rushed to the second strand, and Tynan was going to shout something when the claymores were detonated, sending clouds of steel at the VC, cutting the front ranks into pieces, chopping heads off at the shoulders, legs at the knees, or tearing the enemy soldiers in half. Most of the front rank of the attackers died as the claymores were used, but there were more VC behind them and they took the places of the dead, grabbing the dropped weapons and using them against the Americans.

A drum of foogas went up, exploding in a glowing cloud of flame that engulfed fifteen of the enemy, their dying screams lost in the roar of the weapons. One of them ran the way he had come, a glowing ball of fire that finally fell near the first strand of wire, the light slowly fading.

Tynan flipped his selector switch to full auto and began hosing down the whole area, but the enemy kept coming, screaming and whistling, the bugles urging them forward to kill the American dogs. The bunker next to his, on the side opposite where Duke and Jones and Boone were, exploded in a fiery blast. The Vietnamese swarmed around it, parting like the water of a river as it hit a stone, some of them shooting into the bunker as if to kill the men who were already dead inside it.

Tynan turned and fired into the crowd as it ran by. He shot in short bursts, switching magazines rapidly, watching the enemy soldiers drop as they were hit. Around him he heard the firing of other weapons: rifles, pistols, machine guns. They blended into a continuous roar that Tynan slowly pushed from his mind

until he could no longer hear it. The only sound was
the firing of his own weapon and the hammering of
his heart. Then he heard something hit the wall of the
bunker but thought nothing of it as bullets ripped into
the sandbags, throwing dirt into his face.

"Grenade!" shouted Clayton as he dived over the
side of the bunker.

Tynan and Sterne did the same and were immediately taken under AK-47 fire. Tynan, lying on his
stomach, rolled to the right, firing as the grenade in
the bunker went off and dirt and debris rained down
on his back.

Coming at him, the bayonet on his AK-47 extended,
was a single Viet Cong soldier. Tynan stared at the
enemy for a moment, fascinated by the sight. He fired
once and heard the man grunt as if in pain, but he
didn't slow. Tynan scrambled to his knees, aimed for
the center of the soldier's chest, and shot again. The
oncoming enemy seemed to stumble, then regain his
balance. A long, piecing wail erupted from the VC's
throat as Tynan fired again and again.

The bullets slammed into the enemy soldier who
slipped, stood wavering for a moment, and then
lurched at Tynan, but now it seemed to be an uncon-
scious move. He weaved from side to side, his bayonet nearly dragging in the dirt. He fell to his knees,
turned his head to the right, and collapsed onto his
face.

Clayton suddenly shouted, "Back in the bunker.
Get down. In the bunker." A siren in the center of
the camp began to wail, the sound climbing and falling.

Neither Tynan nor Sterne understood the urgency
in Clayton's voice, but they obeyed, standing and diving back over the sides.

"Keep your heads down!" ordered Clayton.

Then it sounded like the center of the base exploded, and Tynan heard the air filled with a buzzing that disappeared rapidly. It was followed by screams and bodies falling. There was a second burst, and the siren stopped. Clayton looked up and hit Tynan on the shoulder. Tynan saw only a few VC standing inside the wire, and those were weaving back and forth as if sick or drunk. There were a couple of rifle shots and the men fell.

Tynan saw dozens of bodies lying on the ground around him. Each was covered with blood and had a hundred or more darts sticking in him. A few moaned. Many had lost legs or arms or heads. The side of the bunker facing the artillery tubes was full of fléchettes, metal darts an inch and a half long. They were from the beehive rounds that the artillerymen pumped through the tubes as the bunker-line defense collapsed.

Sporadic firing was coming from the line as the GIs shot at the few surviving VC who were trying to flee. There was almost no shooting in return. Just the occasional pop of the enemy mortars as they dropped harassing fire on the camp, but it was poorly aimed.

For an hour, Tynan and Sterne crouched in the bunker, their eyes scanning the territory in front of them. They could see no sign of living enemy. There were hundreds of bodies scattered around them, from the first strand of wire back through the bunker line and almost to the artillery pieces. There was an occasional moan or cry from somewhere out on the field, but there was no movement.

Inside the camp, the medics moved slowly from position to position, treating the men who had been lightly wounded in the fight. The seriously injured had been carried back toward the center of the base where the aid station was set up. Helicopters had already evacuated the critically injured by swooping in under the cover of helicopter gunships and countermortar fire.

Other men moved among the enemy, looking for wounded to make sure that they would cause no more trouble. Those who could be moved were herded toward the center of the camp where a makeshift POW compound had been established. Still other men picked up the weapons scattered around so that the enemy wouldn't be able to retrieve them.

It was almost three in the morning when Riordan appeared at the bunker. He said, "You boys can desert your post now if you want. I don't think we'll be hit again tonight."

Tynan nodded and ejected the round that was chambered. He stood up and leaped over the back wall of the bunker. Sterne did the same, and then all three of them ran back toward the command post. Once there, Sterne went off in search of a cup of coffee and waited for the others while Tynan and Riordan went inside the bunker.

"First thing you need to do," said Riordan, "is make contact with your base. Someone has been trying to reach you on the radio." Riordan consulted a slip of paper. "Call sign of Comet Two."

Tynan set his CAR-15 on the table and took the single sheet of paper as if it contained something more. He wiped the sweat from his forehead with the sleeve of his jungle jacket. He said, "That's naval intelligence in Nha Be."

"Why don't you get on the horn and see what they want," said Riordan, "and I'll check things on the perimeter."

"Wait, Colonel," said Tynan. "What did you mean earlier when you said that you thought it was over for tonight?"

Riordan turned back, facing Tynan. He said, "Simply that it was getting too late for Charlie to launch another assault tonight. If it failed, he would be stuck in the open where everybody could see him. He needs time to go to exfiltrate. He must be going somewhere else, because we sure as hell can't find him during the day. If we could, we might be able to break up his units before they have the chance to organize to hit us."

"Is this over, then?"

"If you mean the attacks tonight, yes. If you mean the attempt to overrun the base, no. He only made one all-out attack, and it failed."

Riordan stepped toward the bunker door and stopped again. "I'll want to check the maps and positions tomorrow, but I think you stopped the real effort. I think the company you hit was supposed to either draw fire or penetrate the base, giving us too much to do. And I'll want to look at the locations where you saw Charlie making his coffins. But, just so you know, without you tonight, we could have been in the hurt locker."

"Thanks, Colonel," said Tynan. He watched Riordan disappear through the door and then moved to the radio. He looked at the piece of paper and thought about the two men on his team who had died. Riordan's comments took some of the sting out of those deaths because his SEALS had provided useful information and a useful service. It was better than dying in a helicopter crash on the way to Saigon for rest and relaxation or falling overboard and drowning. Again, he forced the thoughts from his mind because of the tasks he had yet to perform.

The sergeant there, a young man who had temporarily replaced Meade, handed Tynan a mike and said,

"I've set it for the frequency of your base at Nha Be." He stepped away as Tynan moved close.

Tynan squeezed the mike and said, "Comet Two, this is Black Baron Six."

"Black Baron Six, this is Comet Two," crackled the radio. "Say location."

Tynan hesitated because he had been told not to answer such questions on the radio. All it did was identify the units in the field for the Viet Cong. And Tynan had been given no codes to cover the situation with Comet Two, especially since Comet Two was not in his immediate chain of command.

On the radio he said, "We are secure."

"Roger. Understand. You are ordered to vacate that location at earliest possible opportunity and return here. The orders have been issued by the highest available authority."

"Say again," said Tynan, trying to buy a moment to think.

"You are ordered to return here at first opportunity."

There was no response that Tynan could make. He felt hot and tired and irritated. He was wandering around, trying to do a job, and it seemed that no one wanted him to do it. He was told to put together a team of expert jungle fighters. Men trained in every aspect of the military science. Men who would be at home operating in the jungles of Vietnam, or in the deserts of Iran, or in the rivers of Africa. But somehow he always ran into trouble. Now Commander Walker at Nha Be thought that he had overstepped his authority and was out hunting for the Viet Cong.

Well, that was true, he was hunting the Viet Cong, but that was his job. He listened as the carrier wave crackled and popped with static. He tried to think of something to say, but there was nothing he could do.

"Roger," he hissed finally and tossed the mike at the sergeant.

Outside the bunker, in the fresh air of the early Vietnamese morning, as the stench of the cordite blew away on the light breeze that would soon evaporate, Tynan found Riordan talking to Sterne.

"Colonel," interrupted Tynan, "are you going to get hit again tonight?"

"What do you think?"

Tynan looked at the base again. There were tiny fires burning everywhere. There were bodies everywhere. The observation tower lay on its side, a twisted wreck. Black smoke blew from the bunker line, hiding some of the damage there but also pointing to some of it. In the distance there was the firing of American artillery directed at the suspected VC rally points. Behind him, an Army truck was burning rapidly. There was no reason for the Viet Cong to let up.

"Yeah, I think they will," said Tynan.

"And in force," said Riordan. "Unless we can find out where they're hiding. That's the real key here."

That sparked something in the back of Tynan's mind, but he couldn't put a finger on it. He let it drift back there and waited for it to surface as he knew it would.

8

Tynan watched the chopper that had ferried him from Fire-Support Base Crockett to Nha Be lift off in a cloud of red dust and swirling debris and disappear in the distance. He shouldered the equipment he had brought with him, having left the majority of his field gear at the fire base. He walked off the dock that served as a helipad, turned up the white-fence-lined street, and headed for the intelligence office.

This time Tynan didn't hesitate in Walker's outer office. He nodded at the clerk who was pounding on a scarred typewriter that looked old enough to have been used by Noah to type the manifests on the ark.

The clerk looked up and then started to stand. "You have to be announced," he protested.

"Don't worry about it," said Tynan. "I'm expected."

He threw open the door and then stopped dead in his tracks.

Walker was sitting behind his desk. Seated on it was a Navy nurse, her short skirt hiked up to mid-thigh, revealing her stocking tops and her garter. Walker had one hand on her knee. When she turned, Tynan saw that she had beautiful brown eyes. Her face was thin and she had a dimple in her chin. Her brown hair was pulled back so that it was off her forehead and the collar of her uniform.

"I can come back some other time if you're busy," said Tynan sarcastically.

The nurse smiled at him and then said to Walker, "You take those aspirin, and if you don't feel better by this afternoon, you come by the dispensary."

"Thank you, Ensign," said Walker.

She hopped off the desk, bent at the waist so that she could smooth her stockings, and then tugged at the hem of her skirt. She stopped in front of Tynan and smiled broadly at him, revealing perfect pearly teeth, but said nothing to him.

When she shut the door on her way out, Walker demanded, "What the hell do you mean barging in here like that, Lieutenant?"

For a moment Tynan stood there, staring at Walker, and then he slowly turned and looked at the door almost as if he could still see the ensign. Finally he flopped into the chair, hooked one leg over the arm, revealing a muddy boot, and leaned his CAR-15 against the armrest.

"You called for me," explained Tynan, "and I don't have the time to fuck around."

"Hold your horses, Lieutenant. And you watch your mouth."

Tynan decided that there was no reason to antagonize Walker unnecessarily. He rubbed his hand over his face and realized that he hadn't even removed the camouflage paint. He suppressed a grin, now understanding why the ensign had been smiling at him. It wasn't every day that someone in dirty jungle fatigues wearing camouflage paint walked into the intel office.

He pulled an OD handkerchief from the side pocket of his fatigues and scrubbed at his face, removing most of the camo paint. There were smears of it near his hairline, along his jaw, and on his neck. He leaned back in his chair, stared at the window behind Walker's head, and said, "You called for me, remember?"

Now Walker stood up. He turned his back on Tynan so that he could study something outside. He spun back, slammed a hand to the desktop, and demanded, "Who the hell told you to go fuck around the Hobo Woods?"

"No one told me to. I was carrying out a mission into the area. A fairly routine recon."

"Under whose authority?" yelled Walker, his face a twisted mask.

"The captain of my ship," responded Tynan evenly. "He has the authority over my actions. Not you."

Walker opened the middle desk drawer and took out a piece of paper. He pushed it at Tynan and said, "This is all the authority I need. It places you under the operational control of this office for the next six weeks, and my first order to you is to stay the fuck out of the Hobo Woods."

Tynan leaned forward and grabbed the paper by the corner as if afraid that he would leave fingerprints on it. He read quickly and slipped it back on the desk.

"That paper does not contain enough signatures. Your action is worthless without the approval of the captain of my ship."

Walker sat down again and said, "You really think that I'll have trouble obtaining that, with Captain Masterson's signature on the document?"

"Probably not," agreed Tynan, "but until you do, that paper isn't worth much."

"Then let me put it to you this way, Lieutenant. I'm a commander in the Navy. I outrank you and I am giving you a lawful order. You are to stay out of the Hobo Woods."

Tynan sighed, rubbed a hand through his sweat-damp hair. "Why? I don't understand this at all."

"First, because I said so. Second, you were told not to tell the Army that the Viet Cong were operating in the Hobo Woods until we had confirmation. You ignored that order. Now we want you out of there before you do any more harm."

"Harm?" shouted Tynan. "Harm? I have done no harm. . . ."

"Two of your men are dead."

Tynan rose. He felt the anger rise in him like a firestorm after a bombing raid. He tried to rein in his emotions. At Walker he hissed, "Now, don't you go blaming me for that. They died in combat. I did nothing to get them killed."

"Except order the mission," said Walker smugly.

"Searching for the confirmation that you demanded," countered Tynan. "If you hadn't been so concerned about looking foolish in front of the Army brass, you would have passed along the information. Hell, we could have done it under the table if you wanted to avoid official channels."

"Tynan"—Walker sighed—"I don't know why I bother with you. Let me just say this. Intelligence is a building of credibility. Without credibility, you don't have shit. Bad information loses credibility. Good information builds it. Unsubstantiated information that proves to be false destroys credibility."

"I don't think I believe this."

"The loss of credibility," continued Walker as if he hadn't been interrupted, "means that people stop soliciting my assistance on mission planning, and that eventually is reflected in my promotion jacket."

"Is that all this means to you?" said Tynan, aghast. "A promotion?"

"No. No, of course not. I'm merely explaining the facts of life to you. That we must pass along solid information when we have it, but we must use judgment when the information is less than reliable."

"Fine," said Tynan. "Fine. I understand."

"Good. Now, I want you to pull your people out of the field and prepare for another assignment."

"Whoa," said Tynan. "Let's talk about this. We know that the information I had was good. I spent the night at Crockett as the Viet Cong stormed the wire."

"And did an admirable job," said Walker.

"But there is more to be done there," said Tynan. "Much more."

"I'm sure that the Army can handle it," said Walker. "Why not let them?"

"Why not help them?" asked Tynan. "Looks good in the papers and during review boards if we help. Interservice cooperation. Army gets into trouble and calls on the Air Force to help. The Air Force responds with fighters and transports and resupply. The Navy, on the other hand, pulls its few people out because they have more important things to do."

Walker held up a hand to stop him. "I never said that the mission I had was more important."

"It's what the papers will say," responded Tynan.

"But there is only a handful of you out there."

"Exactly," said Tynan. "And we can provide a real service to the Army by staying out there for another day or two." Again something flashed in the back of Tynan's mind, but he missed it. He turned his attention to Walker.

"You don't even know if the VC will be back," Walker was saying.

Tynan shook his head. "Not true. They didn't even use half a regiment last night. They were just probing for weak spots and trying to buy a cheap victory.

Tonight, or tomorrow night, they're going to hit Crockett with everything they can muster. They will make the real push.''

Now Walker rocked back in his chair. He clasped his hands behind his head and stared at the ceiling where the fan spun lazily. ''You really think this is a good idea?'' he asked.

''Certainly. Looks good to the newspapers too.'' And then Tynan had it. ''Besides, they don't know where the enemy is. They know he's out there, somewhere. If we can stay in the field, we might be able to uncover Charlie's hiding place, and if we do that, then we've provided the one piece of information that the Army needs and doesn't have.'' As he finished speaking he realized that he didn't have it. Riordan had told him that they didn't know where the VC were rallying. There was something else there, but Tynan couldn't quite get it. It had to do with the fact that Riordan didn't know where the VC were forming for the attack. Something he had seen a couple of days earlier.

''All right, Lieutenant,'' said Walker. ''Don't let it be said that I'm unreasonable. You go on back out to Crockett and do what you can to save the Army. I'll expect you back here, in my office, in forty-eight hours.''

Tynan stood and saluted. ''Yes, sir. I'll keep you posted.''

Before he headed back to Crockett, Tynan was tempted to go over to the dining hall for a big breakfast. He smiled as he thought of his men eating cold C rations at Crockett, unless they used one of the fires to heat the cans. Of course, heated C rations were still C rations, and it somehow seemed decadent to be eating real food while his men had to eat the make-believe stuff in C-ration cans.

Then he thought that he had time to fly up to Saigon and see if he could find Bobbi. He hadn't thought about her much during the last few days, but when he had, the feeling of affection had been strong. Seeing her on the TV weather show had been almost too much. And in Saigon, he could find a helicopter heading back into the Hobo Woods. He would have no trouble getting back to the fire base from Saigon.

But that, too, was a bad idea. All he knew about her was that she worked in the embassy during the day. He didn't know if she was just a secretary or if she had some higher, more important job. If she did, he couldn't just barge in on her. He would call her at the embassy the first chance he got.

Then, feeling like a martyr, Tynan decided that he had sacrificed enough for one day and headed for the dining hall. If he couldn't go see Bobbi, he could have a solid breakfast on the Navy. After eating out of OD-colored tin cans, after eating food that tasted like processed cardboard when cold and processed hot cardboard when heated, he was delighted with the dining hall. It was air-conditioned, and it had white table-cloths, white china, and real silverware. There wasn't a line he had to stand in, but waiters who took his order back to the galley. He set his CAR-15 on an empty chair next to him, dropped his gear to the floor under the table, and waited for his real, freshly squeezed orange juice, real eggs scrambled lightly, and toast with grape jelly.

As he sat there, enjoying the moments of relaxation, an officer dressed in clean, heavily starched fatigues approached, stood for a second, and then slipped into the chair next to Tynan. The one without Tynan's CAR-15.

"We usually wash our hands before we eat," said the man.

Tynan stared at the man and then held up his hand and looked at the back of it. There were smudges from the camo paint on it. He saw that there was dirt under his fingernails. He smiled and said, "I spent hours getting my makeup just right and I don't want to spoil it."

The man stood and said, "Yes, well, I thought I would mention it. I can see that it does no good."

Suddenly Tynan was irritated. Here was a man in a combat zone worried because Tynan's hands might be dirty, as if it made any difference to that man. There were more important things to worry about.

"Tell you what," said Tynan, "I'll wash my hands if you'll accompany me into the field."

The man didn't respond. He spun on his heel and walked off, shaking his head as if he were talking to himself.

Tynan chuckled quietly and waited for his food. It arrived a minute later, the steam rising from the eggs. The orange juice was chilled and the grape jelly was nearly perfect. He peppered his eggs and wished that he had ordered hash browns to go with them.

When he finished breakfast, he picked up his weapon and equipment, saw the man who had spoken to him still sipping coffee, and waved to him. "Have fun in the war," said Tynan as his parting shot.

Outside, he headed back to the dock that was the helipad and talked to the clerk there who coordinated the incoming and outgoing flights. He wanted something heading back to Cu Chi at the very least. From Cu Chi, with so many helicopter units operating from the camp including the 116th Assault Helicopter Company, the Three-Quarter Cav, and the aviation battalion that supported the 25th Infantry Division, Tynan figured he could easily get back to Crockett.

Since there was nothing scheduled in or out for a few minutes, Tynan wandered over to the commo room in the headquarters building. He found a field phone and used it to get a call through to the American Embassy in Saigon. He asked to talk with Bobbi Harris and was told that no one by that name worked in the embassy. He thought about it for a second, remembered that her first name was Susan, and asked for Susan Harris. The secretary who answered told him to wait just a moment and she would see if Ms. Harris was free.

A second later Tynan heard the husky voice say, "This is Ms. Harris. May I help you?"

"Sure you can," answered Tynan, smiling to himself.

"Mark? Is that you?"

"None other."

"Let me think," she said quickly. "I've got about ten minutes' worth of work that I absolutely must complete, but then I can get away. I'll let you buy me lunch."

Tynan laughed. "I'd love to buy you lunch, but I'm afraid that it won't be possible."

"Well, why the hell not?"

"I'm not in Saigon. I just called to say hello and see how you're doing." He smiled at the phone, happy that she sounded so happy to hear from him.

"Where are you, then?" she snapped. "Can you get here for lunch?"

"Not today, I'm afraid."

"Oh," she said unhappily, but then went on to tell him about her day and what was going on in the embassy. She finally wound down and asked, "When will you get back to Saigon?"

"A couple of days," said Tynan. "You want me to give you a call?"

"Hell, yes," said Bobbi. She hesitated for a moment and then said, "Wait until you see what I've got planned for you."

"I can't," he said. "Listen, I've got to split. Catch a flight."

"Okay, Tynan," she said. "Catch your flight, but I'm expecting a call from you in a couple of days, and you'd better call."

"Yes, ma'am. Talk to you then." He hung up slowly, staring at the phone. It had gone much better than he had hoped.

Twenty minutes later he was on a chopper heading to Crockett. The pilot had told him it was no big deal to get in during the day. Tynan suspected that the man wanted to see what the base looked like after a night of heavy fighting.

Tynan was met at the pad by Duke and Riordan. Both of them looked hot and tired. Duke kept wiping the perspiration from his face with the sleeve of his fatigues. There were black circles under his eyes. There were dark sweat stains on his uniform and he hadn't shaved. Tynan was tired too but had dozed on the chopper ride from Nha Be, and even though it had been a fairly short flight, he felt refreshed.

"I've a couple of ideas," said Tynan as soon as the helicopter had taken off, "if you would like to hear them. Things that should help."

"Let's go inside," said Riordan tiredly. He nodded toward the command bunker.

Tynan saw Duke hesitate and said, "Paul, come with us."

Inside the bunker, out of the bright sun that was baking the ground, it was cooler. Riordan collapsed into one of the chairs. He took his steel pot off and let it fall to the rough wood floor with a dull thud. He rubbed his face vigorously and said, "I've got to get some sleep before tonight."

"Yes, sir," said Tynan. "I was thinking that you don't need us inside the perimeter. Your troops know what they're doing, and five or six more guns aren't going to help all that much."

Riordan nodded. "You pulling out?"

"No, sir. No way. I'm going to suggest that we, meaning my boys, operate outside the wire. We can make hit-and-run attacks at the rear of the VC formations. We can disrupt them while they are trying to get ready for their assault."

"I don't know about that," said Riordan. "We'll be dropping artillery, calling in air strikes and helicopter gunships. You might get caught in the cross fire."

"There is that danger," agreed Tynan, "but you do have standard tactics, don't you? There are patterns used in those attacks, aren't there?"

"But artillery is a little unpredictable. The powder might burn hot and we get a long round. The fly-boys might misunderstand the instructions and drop their load in the wrong place."

"Still, there are tactics that you use. Ways to predict what is going to happen so that we can avoid being hit by friendly fire."

Riordan leaned forward to the map that was still on the table. He pointed to a large open area near the center and said, "We dropped our base right here. Nearest trees are four hundred meters away. To the north is Fire-Support Base Pershing, to the east are Cu Chi and Fire-Support Base Crazy Horse, and to the south is Fire-Support Base Patton. Now, assuming that the VC assemble in the closest jungle area for the assault, the artillery will be directed against them from the north and south.''

"So," said Tynan, "if we're to the west of them, we'll be safe."

Riordan shot him a glance and then smiled. "Outside the wire, you won't be safe. You just have to remember where the artillery is located and how the patterns will be established for the firing."

"I have a question, sir," said Duke. "Where do you drop the artillery? On them, behind them, or in front of them?"

"Normally we try to drop it right on top of them. Anything else is not effective, and when they're storming the wire, we want to kill them, not herd them."

"So if we're behind them by a couple of hundred meters, we should be relatively safe," said Duke.

"Relatively." Riordan turned his attention back to Tynan. "Just what do you have in mind?"

Now Tynan grinned. "It seems to me that if I set up a bank of claymore mines and triggered them at the rear of the VC formations before fading into the trees, it would thoroughly confuse the enemy. Toss grenades at them. Open fire with our weapons and then take off. Snipe at the officers."

"I'm not sure that it's such a great idea. You'll have your butts hanging out."

"It's what we're trained to do," said Tynan. "We're supposed to be guerrilla fighters, just like the VC. Here is an opportunity to use our training. It's exactly what we should be doing but what everyone tries to prevent us from doing. Besides, you don't know where the hell the VC are massing for the assault. Outside the wire, we might be able to do something about that."

"That's the one thing we'd like to know," agreed Riordan. "If we could drop the artillery on them as they form up, it might keep them out of the wire, and I would much rather that they stayed out of the wire."

"So I'll get my boys some lunch and we'll take off. Outside the wire."

"Well, Lieutenant," said Riordan, "you're not under my control, and if you want to take your people out, then that is up to you."

"What I would like to do," said Tynan, "is take out two two-man teams and leave the fifth guy here with a radio to coordinate our activities. He'll know where we are and can warn us if we're in the gun-target lines or ground zero."

"He may not be able to provide you with much of a warning. Besides," said Riordan, "I don't like giving that information out over the radio."

"Easily fixed, sir," said Duke. "We'll devise a grid system that will be on only three maps. That way if Charlie is listening in, he'll get information that will do him no good."

Riordan stood, bent to retrieve his helmet, holding it against his side and under his arm, and said, "Work out the details and let me know what they are before you leave."

"No problem." Tynan watched as Riordan left the bunker. He knew that the Army colonel had a lot of other problems to deal with. He had to make sure that the bunker line was rebuilt, that the destroyed observation tower was erected, that his men were given some time to sleep and to eat, and he had to do something with the bodies of the VC killed. In the heat of Vietnam it didn't take long for the decomposition of the dead to breed disease, and the last thing they needed was that trouble.

As the colonel left the bunker Duke said, "I imagine that I'll be taking out one of the teams."

"Right," said Tynan, "and I'll have the other. I think we should leave Jones here as the radio liaison. I want someone with some experience handling the job. Someone that we know and can trust."

For the next hour they worked out the details. They would use helicopters to take them into the field. That wouldn't be a problem, because there were helicopters coming in all day with new supplies and equipment. They would take as much as they could, leave it stashed, hidden in the trees or in one of the abandoned villages, and use that as an RP and resupply point. Each team would operate independently of the other, and each would do everything it could to disrupt the VC's attack plans.

Tynan watched as Duke, using a felt-tip marker, drew a grid system over one map, numbered the grids in a random way so that no pattern developed, and then duplicated his map two times. With that done, he and Tynan developed an operating plan establishing the patrol zone for each team. Together, they figured out the best routes for each team to take, sketching them on the maps. The routes would be there so that each team would have an idea about the location of the other in case they needed support.

That done, Tynan told Duke to brief the others and get them ready. He wanted each man to check his weapon and get as many spare magazines as he could carry while he, Tynan, went out to coordinate the effort with Riordan. He made sure that Duke knew they wouldn't need to carry extra socks, C rations, or any of the other things they usually needed for an extended patrol. At the most, they would be in the field for eight or nine hours. That meant that Tynan was going to take as many claymore mines and hand grenades as could be spared. In fact, Tynan thought about getting another M-79 grenade launcher so that each team would have one.

Riordan didn't like giving away the claymores, but the resupply ships had brought so many that they could have ringed the base twice and still not used them all. He told Tynan to search through the stacks of supplies being dropped off and take anything that he thought he could use. Tynan grabbed a couple of the grunts and had them help as he searched through the materiel, putting everything that he wanted to one side. Then they moved it all toward the helicopter landing area. That done, Tynan went back to the command bunker where Duke was cleaning his weapon. The rest of the team was taking care of the last-minute details.

As Tynan entered, Jones approached him. "Skipper, I don't like the way the assignments have been handed out. Anyone can stay here as liaison."

"Tom, I thought about this a long time, and I want you to stay. I trust you to take care of us, especially when things begin to heat up. There is going to be a lot of pressure on the guy who stays here, most of it because he is going to be on the outside looking in and is going to be missing the fight. And he has the toughest job: guarding the radio while his friends are in the field. But I need someone I can trust."

"But, Skipper—"

"But nothing, Tom. Besides, the VC are going to hit the camp. I don't think you need to worry about the war passing you by, if that's what concerns you. You'll be in the thick of things, and when the real assault starts, it may be us on the outside looking in."

Staff Sergeant Meade stepped into the bunker at that point. He looked worn out. He had taken off his helmet and left it somewhere. His fatigues were soaked, as if he had been standing in a shower fully clothed.

He announced, "The colonel has two helicopters waiting to transport you into the field."

"Thank you, Sergeant," Tynan said. He turned to Duke and asked, "Everyone ready to go?"

"Yes, sir." Duke took a step forward and said, "This is your copy of the grid."

Tynan took it, folded it, and stuffed it into one of the pockets of his jungle fatigues. To Jones, he said, "Good luck tonight. I'm counting on you."

Jones said, "Yes, sir, I know. Good luck to you."

"Thanks." He hesitated, looked around the bunker a last time wondering what he had forgotten, and then said, "Let's go, boys."

9

Riordan had ordered two helicopters to stand by so that Tynan and his team could use them. With the help of a couple of grunts, they loaded the claymore mines, the extra ammo, the hand grenades, LAWS, and two XM21 sniper rifles complete with silencers and bipods. Tynan wasn't sure that they would have the opportunity to use them, but he wanted them just in case. They piled everything on the floor of the cargo compartment, starting at the troop seat and working their way forward.

When they were nearly finished, Tynan stepped up on the skid of the lead chopper. "Can you find this ville?"

The pilot reached out through the side window in the door of the chopper and took the map, comparing it with his own. He nodded and shouted back, "Easily. Are there VC near?"

"I don't think so. We swept through the general area yesterday and didn't see anyone."

The pilot touched a couple of places on his map. "We've reports of people taking fire here this morning."

"Anybody got any ideas about enemy movements?"

"No," said the pilot, shaking his head. "We've been in three times and haven't taken fire since early this morning. Seems Charlie has dropped off the face of the earth."

"Good," said Tynan. "Now, after you drop us off, can you buzz a couple of other clearings to confuse anyone who might be watching?"

"Sure." The pilot handed the map back to Tynan. "Whenever you're ready."

Tynan looked back toward the second chopper and saw that Duke and Boone had already climbed on board. He saw Duke hold a hand outside, his thumb up, telling Tynan that he was ready to go. Sterne was already on the troop seat, his feet propped up on a case of hand grenades. Tynan leaped in, slapped the pilot on the shoulder to tell him to take off, and then dropped onto the red canvas seat, ignoring the seat belt. He checked the selector switch on his CAR-15 to make sure that it was on safe.

The roar of the engine increased as the pilot rolled on the throttle. Slowly the helicopter lifted off the ground, swinging back and forth as if suspended below a long wire. It began to turn into the wind, stopped, and then the nose fell forward as the chopper started to race toward the concertina only three feet off the ground.

Tynan looked to the rear and saw the second chopper following close behind. There was a double cloud of dust blowing to both sides as the helicopters raced along the ground. As they approached the perimeter they seemed to rock back and then leaped upward, gaining altitude rapidly.

Once outside the camp and away from the burned-back vegetation of the killing zones, the choppers dropped down to the ground flashing along. They slowed, seemed to hover through a large clearing bordered by trees and filled with low bushes and tall grass. The door gunners opened fire, pouring a stream of M-60 tracers into the tree lines surrounding the field. They popped up again, climbing to a thousand feet before falling toward the ground. They nearly stopped in a tiny clearing, the helicopter turning slowly as if the pilot were looking for something. After making a full 360-degree turn, he dumped the nose, charged a tree line, and popped over it.

Tynan felt a tap on his shoulder. The crew chief leaned close, shouting into his ear, "We're going to land in your LZ on the next letdown. Be ready."

Tynan shouted at Sterne, "Get set." He then checked his weapon, made sure a round was chambered, and set it back on safe. He watched Sterne do the same thing and then tugged at the big Randall combat knife to make sure that it was secured.

Again the helicopter fell to the ground, flared back, and then the skids touched the earth. Tynan leaped out, quickly checked the surroundings, and then turned back so that he could help the crew chief, who was pushing the boxes of ammo and equipment from the cargo compartment.

In seconds, both helicopters were gone, climbing into the afternoon sun, their door guns hammering at the trees under them until they were out of sight. Tynan was down on one knee, using the boxes for cover as he surveyed the hootches and palms near him. He saw no movement anywhere. He pointed to the left and then at Duke and Boone, telling them to swing in that direction.

With Sterne, Tynan advanced toward a hootch. There was bright sunlight shining on the door so that they could see some of the interior. The thatch on the roof was old and rotting and had fallen away in a couple of places, revealing disintegrating rafters.

Tynan hit the wall with his shoulder, causing the mud to cascade to the ground. He glanced around the corner, but inside there was nothing except a single dirty bamboo mat and the broken bottom of an earthen pot.

Tynan glanced at Duke, who was emerging from another hootch, shaking his head to tell Tynan that it was empty. Tynan then entered the hootch, kicked the mat aside to see if it concealed a trapdoor that would lead into a tunnel system or a family bunker. When he didn't find anything under the mat, he searched along the walls, looking for a door that could hide the bunker, but the walls were solid. He used the butt of his CAR-15 to tap them, and although they weren't sturdy, they were solid, concealing no secrets.

He stepped into the sunlight and said, "We'll use this as our rally point. Let's get the equipment inside."

They formed a human chain and tossed the boxes from one to the other while Duke disappeared inside periodically to stack them. In only a few minutes they moved the equipment from the landing zone to the hootch. That done, Tynan told Sterne to make a circuit of the ville, and to keep an eye open.

Inside the hootch, Tynan and Duke began opening the boxes and setting out the equipment. Claymores in one area, grenades in another, and ammo in the third. Tynan picked up the M-14 sniper rifle, pulled the caps off the scope, and sighted through it a couple of times. The problem was that neither he nor Duke had had a chance to zero the weapon, and if they wanted to snipe at long range, they couldn't be sure that the round would fly true. At shorter ranges, under four hundred meters, they could probably hit what they aimed at. Over four hundred the rounds might only wing the target.

Next Tynan checked both the radios. It was imperative that they both worked. Once he had checked in with Jones at Crockett, he turned them off for a few moments.

Sterne returned and said, "I didn't see anything. Looks like this place has been deserted for a long time. Dung piles in the water-buffalo pens have dried up. Well at the far end is dry too. There are weeds growing in a couple of the hootches."

Tynan nodded during Sterne's report and then said, "Let's load up." He helped Sterne pick up the PRC-25 radio and strap it on. Next he assisted Sterne with claymore mines, loading him down with them. Sterne began packing hand grenades everywhere that he could, stuffing them into his pockets and slipping the safety handles into the holes in his web gear. Finally he took a couple of bandoliers of ammo.

Tynan took a number of claymores, loading them into his pack since it held nothing else. He, too, picked up grenades. He slung the sniper's rifle over his shoulder along with a couple of extra magazines for it. He also carried his CAR-15 and both his pistols. Like Sterne, he picked up a couple of bandoliers so that he would have all the ammo he would need. Neither he nor Sterne could carry the M-79 or the 40mm grenades for it.

Duke and Boone picked up their equipment. Duke opted to take the M-79 and leave the sniper rifle behind. He thought that the Willy Pete, high explosive, and canister rounds for the M-79 would be more useful than the XM-21. He made sure that they had a number of the claymores and extra grenades. When he had everything he wanted, he stood and asked, "What rules are we operating under?"

"Kill the gooks," said Tynan. "As quickly and as many as you can. That, and find out where they're hiding. If we can find the rally points, we can break up the advance on Crockett.''

"Yes, sir." Duke tapped Boone on the shoulder and pointed at the door. They exited, turned to the south, and disappeared from sight quickly, using the palm and coconut trees for cover.

"Well?" said Sterne.

Tynan looked at the equipment, checked what they had taken again, and then said, "Let's go."

Outside, they turned to the south, just as Duke had done, but once away from the ville, they turned to the east. They entered the trees, Sterne in front, chopping at the brush and vines with his machete. They switched off periodically because the sun seemed to sap their strength and neither of them could maintain the pace for long. Sweat poured off them.

Tynan kept a close watch on his map, checking the landmarks, the streams, the abandoned villages and plantations of the Hobo Woods. He could hear the helicopters working the area, taking supplies to Crockett, but he wasn't quite close enough to see them. In the far distance he could hear artillery firing but could tell that it was not from Crockett by the direction. Consulting the map, he decided that he was about a klick or a klick and a half from Crockett. He halted and waited for Sterne to approach.

"We'll set up here," he said. "We won't put out the claymores, except for a couple to cover a retreat if we have to bug out. Once we see how this is going to break, we'll make plans."

Behind him Tynan could see a couple of tall trees. One of them had a fork in the trunk about fifteen feet above the ground. The foliage around it was thick, and he figured it would be the perfect place for a sniper.

He pointed at it and said, "I'm going up there for a while. I'll be able to see what's going on out there and maybe take out a target of opportunity."

"Yes, sir."

Tynan hesitated, took a couple of the claymores, and arranged them so that they protected him in the tree. He set them in a circle about fifteen meters away, facing away from the tree. He ran the firing cables from them and set them at the base of the tree. He then climbed up and found that, by leaning back, he could brace himself against the tree so that he was sitting forward, the barrel of the rifle on a branch in front of him. He couldn't have found a better perch if he had built it himself.

He watched as Sterne searched the ground around them. He then moved back into a large bush, crawling under it. When he finally made it, Tynan could not see him. He hoped the camouflage was as effective on the ground.

Duke and Boone walked rapidly, keeping at it until both were sweating heavily and breathing hard. They pressed on, through the trees, across an open field filled with rice paddies, and back into the trees. They passed an abandoned hootch, the metal roof full of holes from shrapnel and bullets, the mud walls decaying, and the wooden door lying in the dirt. They thought about using it as a secondary rally point, but they were getting too close to Crockett. The VC would probably rally to it after the attack if they failed to take the base.

Just as they were about to walk away from it, Duke grinned and held up a hand. "Wait one," he said.

Boone dropped to the ground, his weapon pointed to the front, the sweat dripping from his face. He didn't say a word.

Duke took one of the claymores from his pack and looked around. There didn't seem to be a good place for it. He entered the hootch and set it up in one corner, digging it in so that it was pointed slightly upward. He set the mousetrap pull release and ran a wire from it to the side of the hootch. He figured that if he put the tripwire across the doorway, he would kill only one or two of the enemy, but if he set it up out of the way, somebody might stumble into it while there were ten, twelve, or fifteen people in the way.

When he finished, he left the hootch and picked up Boone, and they started off again, working their way closer to Crockett. Finally they found a good place to hide. Good cover for them, but little for the enemy. They crouched down, their feet touching as they faced different directions. It was an old Special Forces trick that prevented the VC from sneaking up on them. They would wait for dark and see where the enemy was before deciding on their next course of action.

At Crockett, Jones sat outside the command post and watched the activity around him. The grunts were in the field, restringing the wire and replacing the claymores. In the bunkers, they were performing maintenance on the weapons, changing the barrels that had scorched or burned up during the firefight. They replaced the ammo and added more. They carried grenades to the bunkers. And while they did all that, others tried to set up a second line of defense. They were throwing up a wall of sandbags near the revetments that surrounded the 105s.

A bulldozer had been brought in and had scooped a shallow trench just outside the wire. Men were carrying the bodies of the dead VC out to it and dumping them into it.

As the sun dropped closer to the horizon Jones checked the radio a last time. He wanted to be sure that it was working when things began to pop. He leaned back against the sandbagged wall of the command bunker and slowly took his rifle apart, cleaning each piece of it before giving it a light coating of oil and reassembling it. He got to his feet then, wiped the sweat from his face and hands, and walked to the ammo dump. In it he found several bandoliers of M-16 rounds and picked them up. There were a couple of dozen empty magazines there, and Jones picked them up. He took them back to the command bunker so that he could load them. Just one more way to prepare for the VC.

Tynan used his scope to sweep the surrounding area. Even as the sun fell toward the horizon Tynan hoped to spot someone. Then, at the extreme range of his weapon, he thought he saw movement. He held the scope steady and waited. A second later, he saw it again, and then a third time. He watched as the shape that was little more than a shadow grew, twisted, and then solidified into something that was vaguely human. Moments later he saw another and another, until he discovered every member of the enemy platoon as it slowly worked its way into position.

Tynan thought it strange that he had not been able to see them before they found their staging point. He believed that he could have seen them as they slipped into the field, and then decided that they must have approached through the trees nearly a klick away. Still, it seemed as if they were growing out of the ground.

Slowly the VC disappeared as they dropped to the ground to wait for the signal to attack. Tynan kept his scope moving along the trees and bushes where the enemy crouched. He saw a man get to his feet and walk along the line, apparently talking to each member of the platoon. He would stand near the other VC, his head slightly bowed. Tynan set the cross hairs on the man's back, waited for him to stop, and squeezed the trigger. He felt the rifle fire, felt it jump back into his shoulder, but heard only the quietest puffing sound from the bullet. The operating of the bolt made more noise than the slug. Tynan knew that no one would hear it.

A second later the man seemed to stagger and then fall, crimson blossoming on his back. For a moment there was no movement among the enemy troops because no one knew what had happened. There had been no gunshot, and as far as they knew, there were no Americans around.

A man in a khaki uniform appeared and walked to where the first victim lay. He stooped down, put his hand on the man's back, and then looked at his palm. He turned slightly, his eyes on the trees near them. Slowly he searched the area. Tynan centered the cross hairs and fired again. The man pitched forward to his hands and knees, shaking his head carefully as if to clear it. Then he simply collapsed and lay still.

There was a brief flurry of firing, but none of it was directed at Tynan. The VC were just spraying around some bullets, unsure of what had happened or how it had happened. They were hoping for some kind of response so that they could find the man who was shooting at them.

Through the scope, Tynan could barely see the face of one of the enemy. He sighted his weapon, the cross hairs just below the chin, and fired. He saw nothing happen and thought that he had missed. Then he saw a flash of reflected sunlight as the man dropped his rifle. Tynan saw the body tumble forward, but it disappeared into the thick bush nearby.

There was a sudden flurry of activity from the VC. Several of them stood up and ran for the nearest tree line. They disappeared into it. A couple of others ran in the other direction and began sweeping toward Tynan's hiding place. He could see them clearly as they dodged around the trees and bushes. They seemed to have no idea of what they were doing. He shifted his weight so that he could swing his rifle. He aimed carefully at the man who seemed to be leading the group. Through the scope, Tynan could see him easily. The man wore a soft cap over rather long black hair. He had the beginnings of a beard on his chin. Sunlight reflected from the metal of the collar tabs. In one hand he carried a pistol and in the other a Chicom grenade.

Tynan waited until they had moved to within three hundred meters. Then he positioned the cross hairs on the man's chest, took half a breath and held it. He squeezed the trigger and felt the weapon recoil. The man suddenly dropped both pistol and grenade, took a step backward, and sat down. His right hand clutched at his chest as he slumped to his side.

The men around him dived to the ground and fired a couple of rounds. Then two of them grabbed the fallen VC under the armpits and began dragging him back the way they had come. Two more joined them, backing slowly, their weapons pointed into the trees. Tynan decided that to shoot again would be foolish.

Tynan reached up and wiped the sweat from the side of his face. He felt some of it drip into his eyes, stinging slightly. He searched for another target, away from the retreating patrol, but the sun had fallen too far and the shadows of the trees and bushes made it impossible to see anything easily. And he was afraid that someone in the enemy camp would see his muzzle flash, which in bright daylight was nearly invisible but in the onrushing twilight stood out like a beacon pointing directly at him.

He slung the rifle and dropped lightly to the ground. He crouched there for a moment and then moved toward Sterne. "It's about time for the festivities to begin," he said, the excitement in his voice unmistakable.

10

It had been dark for nearly two hours when Tynan finally heard a distant noise that suggested someone moving through the jungle nearby. Overhead, the clouds had moved in again, masking the stars and hiding the moon. The air had cooled and it smelled like it would rain soon.

Tynan eased his CAR-15 forward, flipped off the safety, and waited. He stared into the night, looking for the enemy, but the VC were well disciplined and he heard only an occasional sound from them. He suddenly felt sweat pop out on his body and bead on his forehead. He wanted to wipe it away and wanted a drink from his canteen, but he refused to move. The enemy was too close.

Tynan took a deep breath and let it out slowly, forcing himself to relax. He closed his eyes momentarily so that he could focus his attention on his hearing, but the enemy soldiers made no more sound. In the distance was the faint booming of artillery as it fired on other targets, and just at the edge of his senses he could hear a single chopper.

He felt a slight pressure on his foot, telling him that Sterne was still there and was aware that the enemy was approaching. Tynan licked his lips slowly and tried to see the VC.

Then, nearly in front of him, he heard a quiet voice speaking Vietnamese, giving orders. He saw a couple of dark shapes flash by, and a third that stood, turned, and disappeared into the deep grass directly in front of him.

There was a rustling as the enemy soldiers began to filter in, taking positions, spreading out, getting ready. Three or four men—Tynan couldn't be sure how many there were because they kept disappearing into the gloom—roamed the rear of the formation, whispering orders and preparing. One man, his voice barely quieted, was talking to individual soldiers, almost like the coach before the big game trying to inflame their emotions.

From the left came more noise as more men filtered in and joined those already there. Tynan tried to keep count, but the shifting shadows and the darkness of the night made it impossible. He guessed that there were two hundred fifty to three hundred men now squatting in the grass twenty meters away.

The noise died down and the men who had been roaming the rear of the formations suddenly disappeared. There was a distant popping and two flares bloomed over Crockett, but they were too far away to give much light to Tynan. He could see a couple of men crouching in the grass, but they were vague shapes and Tynan wouldn't have known they were men if he hadn't heard them speaking quietly to one another.

Tynan slipped backward so that he could talk to Sterne. He moved slowly, carefully, taking his time until he was even with Sterne's feet. He whispered, "We set the claymores in the grass about five meters away and withdraw. I'll punch off the claymores, and then you toss the grenades."

Sterne made no comment. He just began to move forward. He picked up a couple of the claymores and crawled to the left, quickly disappearing into the darkness.

Tynan took three of them and began to ease toward the enemy. He set one up, bracing it against the rotting wood of a fallen palm tree. He set the leads and then crawled to the right, setting up a second.

As he was about to move off he heard a noise, froze, and looked up in time to see a VC soldier walking toward him. Tynan's first thought was that he had somehow been discovered, and then he realized the man would have just shot him if he had suspected anything. Tynan buried his face in the dirt, breathing shallowly. He felt sudden pain in his hand as the VC stepped on his fingers. He glanced up, but the enemy didn't realize what had happened. The soldier continued walking, disappearing into the trees to the far right.

Tynan's first reaction was to follow him and kill him silently, but then he decided that he would only give himself away. Instead, he pushed himself backward, until he was lying next to a large bush. He kept his eyes open and waited patiently, and a moment later the man reappeared.

As soon as he rejoined the company, Tynan finished connecting the leads. He moved again, placed the third mine, and then worked his way back, toward the bush where Sterne waited. As he crawled under, carefully playing the lead wire out, he saw that the enemy was getting ready to leave.

When it was dark out, Jones moved his radio into the command bunker, attached the antenna to one of the lead wires outside so that he would be able to pick up the signals from Tynan and Duke. He tried to stay out of the way so that Sergeant Meade and Colonel Riordan could work without falling over him. He listened as others brought in reports suggesting that the VC were on the move, that there were buildups south of camp, west of camp, and east of camp. He watched the steady stream of people in and out of the command bunker, some of them nearly vibrating with nervousness, others speaking in voices that were too loud, unable to stand or sit quietly.

Jones turned up the gain on his radio, turned up the volume, and then checked his weapon as he waited. He heard the 81mm mortars fire and ran outside, dragging his radio, as the illumination shells exploded high over the base, casting their eerie yellowish light. He looked toward the south where the major buildup was supposed to be taking place, but he could see nothing there except the trees and bushes. He glanced up at the newly erected observation tower but could see no one in it.

The mortars fired again as the parachute flares fell close to the ground. Jones could watch their progress as they floated down, leaving a yellowish trail of smoke as they oscillated beneath the parachutes. The almost-nonexistent wind did not blow the smoke away, and the humidity of the impending rain seemed to strengthen it.

There was a single shot from the bunker line, an overanxious grunt firing at a shadow, then a burst from one of the .50-caliber machine guns. Jones watched the ruby tracers bounce across the landscape and ricochet into the sky, but there was no immediate return fire.

Again there was the pop of the mortars, only this time the sound drifted to them from a long distance. Someone yelled, ''Incoming.''

Jones turned toward the voice and then saw an explosion among the 105s as the first of the enemy mortar rounds impacted. A moment later there was a second and a third as the rounds walked among the howitzers, causing no damage in the heavily sand-bagged revetments.

There was a whoosh overhead and a loud, solid bang as the first of the 122mm rockets hit the base. It landed long, bursting in the helicopter landing area, and did no damage, but when it exploded, it threw out hundreds of jagged pieces of shrapnel that sliced through the night air. The rockets, poorly aimed and with no internal guidance, began raining down, det-onating all over the camp. Their bursts were punc-tuated with mortars that landed amidst the command bunker, the commo bunker, the mess hall and admin bunker, and the observation tower.

Jones watched the first few detonate, fascinated by the fountains of sparks that marked the explosions inside the perimeter, but when they began moving closer to him, he dodged back into the command bunker. As he entered he heard the first roar of Crock-ett's 105s as they responded to the mortars and rock-ets, the single man in the observation tower spotting for them.

"Be a while before they hit us," said Riordan. "They always try to soften us up with a little artillery before they begin the big sweep across the field."

"Sir," said Meade from his post next to the base's radios. "Patton is taking rocket fire, and Crazy Horse reports sappers in the wires."

For a moment Riordan didn't say a word, as if that didn't matter because they all knew the real attack would be against Crockett. "They're trying to bleed off our support," he said. "Can they fire in support of us?"

"Yes, sir, but right now Patton is firing counter-mortar."

Outside, Jones heard the continued detonation of rockets and mortars as the VC gunners began throwing everything they had at Crockett. The explosions of the enemy weapons mixed with the firing of the 105s and the base's 81mm mortars in a duel for supremacy.

"Won't be long now," mumbled Riordan.

In the distance, Duke could hear the firing of the artillery and could see the flares over the base. There was a far-off rumbling that sounded like thunder, but Duke knew that it was mortars and rockets and 105s being shot by both sides. He could see an occasional flash, almost like lightning, as one of the artillery shells exploded in the air.

Around him there was nothing. He had seen no movement of VC or NVA. He had heard nothing. The enemy rocket and mortar positions were in the distance, on the other side of the camp. He was in the wrong place but didn't want to move now. He knew that the VC sometimes blew up one side, or just one bunker on a line, poured through the crack in the defense, and destroyed as much as they could and killed as many as they could as they swept through the base and blew up another bunker to escape. Duke might be in the wrong place at the beginning of the attack, but he could be in the right one as it ended.

When the firing began, the men in the field in front of Tynan crouched down, as if afraid that the shells would fall among them. He heard them talking quietly, the sound barely audible above the night noise of the woods, the animals scurrying about, the faint cries of the nocturnal birds, and the pounding of the artillery.

Tynan picked up the firing controls and glanced toward Sterne. Sterne carefully pulled the pin on a grenade and nodded. With a single motion, Tynan fired the claymore mines in sequence, starting at the left. The first bang was disguised by all the artillery firing at Crockett and there was no reaction from the VC, but then the screams of pain broke through and panic started. Then the mines were firing too fast, and before there was time for much reaction, Sterne was tossing grenades.

As they exploded, both Tynan and Sterne were on their feet, slipping backward, watching the confusion of the VC. Random firing broke out, the shots directed all around. Tynan dived to the ground as a green tracer flashed by. Sterne threw another grenade that exploded to the front of the VC unit. That seemed to draw their attention, and they began to fire in that direction.

Tynan climbed to his feet and both he and Sterne drifted to the rear, at first walking carefully, trying to avoid making noise. Then, feeling that they were far enough away, they turned to run, first due west and then to the north, heading more or less toward the rally point. When they were clear of the area, they slowed and began to search for a new ambush site.

At Crockett, the barrage of enemy weapons lifted abruptly. There was a sudden increase in the intensity of the VC rockets and then a silence. A lone bugle sounded far to the east and was answered by the slow, deliberate chatter of a .50-caliber machine gun. Then to the south came the wail of another bugle and another.

Jones strayed outside the command bunker to take a look. As he stepped from it there was a gigantic crash that sounded like all the artillery in South Vietnam had fired simultaneously and the clouds opened

up. Rain poured from them. There had been no sprin-
kles or light rain. One second it was dry, and the next
everything and everyone was soaked. The rain fell so
hard that it became a gray curtain that obscured the
base, the bunkers, and the enemy soldiers.

Firing erupted around the bunker line as the grunts
lost sight of the wires and then the other bunkers. To
the south, there were shouts and whistles and bugle
calls. The crashing rain concealed the noise, deadened
it, and seemed to shift it around.

There was a single bright flash as the repaired wire
of the perimeter defense exploded. A gap nearly fifty
meters wide was created, but the men on the bunker
line couldn't see that. They just knew that there had
been an explosion close to them. They poured rifle
and machine-gun fire into the gray rain, creating fog
around them, but they had no targets.

A second detonation eliminated the second strand
of perimeter wire, and a third destroyed the last of
that defense. A panicky corporal in one of the bunkers
directly in front of the gap punched the controls for
the claymore mines near him, but that didn't slow the
tide of the VC. Those who were killed fell while those
behind them stepped on the bodies and picked up the
dropped weapons.

A drum of foogas erupted, engulfing an assault
squad in flame, and the heavy rain spread the jellied
gasoline, lighting part of the line. A few VC were
silhouetted by the flaming liquid and were shot down,
but the majority of the enemy avoided the light.

Jones heard the siren in the center of the camp go
off and knew that they were about to lower the tubes
and fire the beehive rounds. That had broken the
assault the night before by raking a whole side of the
perimeter with a curtain of steel.

The artillery fired, the flashes of the howitzers lighting the camp like giant strobes. Jones could see nothing in the light. Everyone seemed to have dropped to the ground as the 105s went off.

Then to the west there was a rising shout and the night was filled with bugles. Firing erupted and green tracers flashed into the base. Again the perimeter defenses exploded and the bunker line returned the fire, but the rain had not slackened and no one could see the enemy.

The man in the observation tower could see only the occasional flash as the bangalore torpedoes took out sections of the wire. He could see no one and tried to direct the firing of the 105s, but it did little good.

The 81s continued to pump out the illumination rounds, but they were reduced to points of light rocking in the sky until their parachutes were so saturated with water that they collapsed. The flares plummeted to the ground, the magnesium in them sputtering and hissing in the rain.

There was rapid firing on the bunker line and shouts raised in both Vietnamese and English. Commands shouted back and forth. Single shots. Shouts of pain. Screams from the dying. Jones scrambled to the edge of the command bunker, looked around, but the rain was falling too hard. He saw a shadowy shape but didn't shoot because he didn't know if it was friend or foe.

Jones spun and ran into the command bunker. "They're in the perimeter," he shouted.

Riordan turned and looked at him. In a voice marked with surprise, he said, "I think they may just overrun us."

The heavy rain finally drove Duke from his ambush position. He had seen absolutely nothing in the hours he had been hiding there and now couldn't even see Boone, who was lying near him. He could hear the firing at Crockett and knew that the attack was on the way.

He drew back, heading to the south. Boone was with him. They kept moving, hurrying toward the hootch where he had rigged the booby trap. The rain was pelting down, splashing back up, the noise from it, along with the firing in the distance, becoming a roar that eliminated every other sound.

Suddenly Duke ran right into the middle of a VC squad. The dozen men were facing away from Duke. He slid to a halt, his first reaction to escape back into the woods before the enemy spotted him, but instead he dropped to the ground as he grabbed a grenade. Boone fell beside him.

When the grenade exploded, Duke was up, firing his rifle at anything he could see. The Viet Cong tried to fight back, but they were confused, surprised by the sudden attack at their rear.

One of them ran at Duke, his bayonet extended in front of him. Duke stood his ground and hesitated and then fired a shot. The round hit the Viet Cong in the chest and staggered him, but the forward motion of his body carried through. The enemy dropped nearly at Duke's feet, his bayonet sticking in the ground inches from Duke's boot.

Boone had backed up so that he was facing in the opposite direction. He saw something move in the distance and fired at it. There was a scream of pain and surprise and then a howl as if the VC hit by Boone's bullet were infuriated. The shape turned, still screaming, and ran at Boone. He fired again and again until the VC stopped screaming and fell, but the enemy soldier wasn't through. He crawled forward on hands and knees, the sounds almost dying in his throat now.

Boone fired a final round into the top of the enemy's head.

Duke took a step forward and caught a flash to his right. He spun and fired. A shot rang out and Duke felt something lance through his side. There was a warm wetness spilling onto his hip, mixing with the cold of the rain. He knew that he had been hit, the pain flaring intensely, radiating upward and outward. He clenched his teeth and fired a burst into the trees. There was no answering fire.

Slowly Duke turned back and tried to see the enemy, but the rain still obscured everything. He took a step forward, felt suddenly dizzy and sick. His knees were weak and he was light-headed. He sat down with an audible grunt as his legs buckled under him. He felt himself falling back and didn't know what was happening.

Tynan had decided to return to the hootch where they had stored their extra equipment and swap the XM-21 for the M-79 since it would be more useful in the heavy rain.

Sterne shouted at him, "Hold it." He stopped and then moved over so that he was crouched near a large tree.

"What is it?"

"Radio message from Jones," Sterne answered. "Artillery coordinates." A moment later he said, "I think we'd better turn to the east. They're going to start dropping artillery all over the fucking place."

"Troop concentrations?" asked Tynan.

"They have no idea. Rain's too heavy and the VC are in the wire now. They're just going to saturate the area and hope for the best."

The rain began to let up. Tynan wiped a hand across his wet face. "I take it to mean that they are getting no pressure from the east."

"Jones just said they were going to fire on the south and west sides of the base."

Then, almost as if to punctuate his words, the first of the rounds burst about half a klick away. They didn't see the flashes but heard the detonations.

"We'd better get going," said Tynan, climbing to his feet.

Jones had just finished telling Sterne about the coming barrage when there was a loud bang that rocked the bunker. Jones threw his hands to his ears and sat down on the floor as dirt cascaded down around him. A second later there was another, more powerful crash that smashed Jones to the floor. He felt as if a giant weight had settled on his chest. Dust filled the air, and he could hear Meade groaning. Somewhere else Riordan was coughing loudly. The lights went out.

Jones rolled to his right, to his hands and knees, and reached out, searching for his rifle. There was a sputtering pop in the corner, and he could see sparks flashing in one of the battery-operated radios.

A beam of light stabbed out, a bright line illuminating the swirling dust. A hand grabbed him and lifted and a husky voice asked, "You okay?"

"Fine," he choked out. "What happened?"

"Satchel charge on top of the bunker."

Jones closed his eyes and nodded. When he opened them he saw large brown spots scurrying from the light beam and thought that he was seeing things. A second light joined the first, and Jones suddenly realized that he was looking at spiders. Giant spiders, almost a foot in diameter, forced out of hiding by the explosions. They were now frantically searching for new crevices.

"Christ!" said Jones, leaping backward. "Jesus Christ!" He started to reach out again, to search for his rifle, but could see nothing in the dark. The last thing he wanted to do was touch one of the hairy creatures. He stood still, suddenly afraid to move his feet, afraid that he might step on one.

Now a third light joined the first two. Jones grabbed the man as he entered the bunker and said, "Help me find my rifle."

The beam began to sweep the floor, but the spiders were gone and Jones wondered if he had imagined them. He found his rifle and picked it up, worked the bolt, and heard the dirt grinding in it. He looked at the radio and saw that a broken beam from the ceiling had smashed it.

"I'm getting out," he said, then ran for the door, wondering again about the spiders. Outside, the rain washed the dust from his face quickly. He coughed again, the dust and dirt thick in his throat. He leaned back against the wet sandbags to get his breath and orient himself. Men were swarming all over the bunker, and there was firing going on. Jones wasn't sure what was happening.

Off to the right there was a crash as the artillery fired again. Slowly he became aware of the rattling of the small-arms fire. He looked up, saw that the rain was no longer the thick fog it had been. He worked the bolt of his rifle again, ejecting a live round, but the grit seemed to have fallen free. He flipped the selector to the five-shot burst position and forced himself up, away from the collapsing walls of the command bunker.

As he ran toward the artillery pieces where the second line of defense was, another explosion knocked him flat. He rolled to the side, looked back, and saw that the command bunker was now a smoking pile of rubble with a dozen tiny fires burning briefly until the rain drowned them. He had gotten out just in time. He got to his feet and staggered to the low sandbag wall that surrounded the 105s.

Tynan and Sterne worked their way through the trees, dodging right and left, listening. Behind them they heard the continual rumble of the artillery as it rolled over the land, searching for the enemy troop concentrations. They hurried on.

Sterne stopped short of a clearing. He crouched at the edge of the trees because he had nearly tripped over a body. He had reached down, taken the AK-47 from the dead fingers. He dropped the assault rifle and felt along the throat, trying to find a pulse, but put his hand into a hole that seemed big enough to drive through. He stared down at his bloody fingers and saw that the VC had taken a round in the neck that had blown out a chunk of flesh three inches in diameter. He could also see that the dead man had lost an ear, an eye, and most of his jaw.

Tynan approached and whispered, "What's the trouble?"

"Dead man. One of theirs."

Then they heard the voices. At first it was just a quiet mumble of words that were unintelligible. But as they listened they picked up a couple of words that were obviously English.

"You think it's Duke?" asked Sterne.

"Paul?" called Tynan softly.

"That you, Lieutenant?" came the response a second later.

Tynan stood and stepped into the clearing. He saw one man crouched over another. He moved close and said, "What the hell?"

"Duke caught one in the side," said Boone. "It's not real serious yet."

"We've got to move," said Tynan. "They're going to start dropping artillery all over this place in a few minutes."

Jones nearly fell over the sandbag wall. He was grabbed by a pair of hands that jerked him over and pushed him to the ground. The voice hissed, "Keep down, you fucking idiot. You wanna die?"

Jones rolled over, got to his knees, and wiped the mud from the front of his fatigues. He peeked over the top of the sandbags and could see shapes moving through the gray mist. He didn't know if they were Americans or the enemy, so he didn't fire at them. And he realized that the rain had slowed down and was beginning to dissipate.

There was firing from the bunker line in the south and east, but none from the west. Jones suspected that the men guarding the 105s were the survivors from the west side of the camp. He didn't say anything to them, just kept his eyes open.

Overhead, a flare burst and the light penetrated to the ground but only added to the riot of shadows and shapes. Jones saw a short man wearing a ragged uniform and a pith helmet and was convinced that it was an NVA soldier. He fired a shot, missed, and fired again. The shape vanished, falling down.

Around him others were now shooting as the enemy began to probe toward them. A Chicom grenade landed in front of the sandbags and Jones ducked, but the weapon failed to detonate. Another landed at the feet of the man next to him, and he picked it up, tossing it back. It didn't explode either.

A satchel charge flew over the wall, hitting fifteen or twenty feet behind him. Jones dropped to the ground, covering his ears and opening his mouth, but someone grabbed it and flung it back at the enemy. It exploded as it landed among the VC.

There were bugle calls then, shouts in Vietnamese, and a surging charge across the open space between the destroyed bunker line and the redoubt. The enemy weapons fired at them, the muzzle flashes lost in the mist but the green tracers bursting through. The men near Jones returned the fire, single shot, until a line of the enemy loomed out of the mist. Jones flipped the selector switch to automatic and held the trigger down, burning through the whole magazine in seconds.

An M-60 machine gun opened fire near him, the rapid chattering punctuating the fight. There was a shout then. "Short burst, asshole. You'll burn up the fucking barrel."

All around, Jones could hear the artillery exploding. The shells were pouring in from the other bases now that they had beaten back the diversions directed at them. Fire control had been taken over by the commo bunker as far as Jones knew. He didn't know if it still existed or not. The other camps might be firing based only on the last information supplied them. But they were throwing a lot of steel into the battle.

As the first attack faltered and broke, the VC scrambling for cover, leaving their dead piled in heaps and their wounded crying for help, Jones wondered where they were coming from. He didn't see how anything could survive in the no-man's-land created by the artillery.

* * *

Together with Boone, Tynan carried Duke out of
the clearing and into the trees. They stopped for a
moment while Tynan examined the wound. He could
see both the entrance and the exit holes and the bleeding had been heavy, but that was a good sign. That
would clean the wound. Duke would need a doctor
soon, but he could walk a short distance. Tynan
decided to try to get them closer to Crockett and then
lie low until the shooting stopped and he could call
for a medevac.

They worked their way through the trees and halted
at the edge of a huge clearing. In the distance they
could now see the flashes of the artillery firing from
Crockett, or else of the mortars and rockets hitting it.
The rain had become little more than a fine mist and
seemed to shimmer in the light of the flares.

Tynan studied the field in front of them. There were
bushes scattered about and tall grass that seemed to
carpet the ground. At first he could see no one at all.
Then a man stood up, walked toward the trees, and
disappeared. A second later he did it again, as if he
were rallying his troops. Tynan smiled, figuring that
he had found the assembly point for the reinforcements in the attack.

When the man stood a third time, Tynan was ready.
He had unslung his sniper rifle and tried to sight
through the scope, but there simply wasn't enough
light. The rain mist was too dense and the flares too
far away to do any good. Instead he used the night-
firing technique he had learned from the Army. Use
both eyes to sight over the barrel, and don't use the
scope. As the enemy soldier stood Tynan fired twice,
the silent cough of the weapon lost in the noise from
the battle at Crockett.

Just like the first time he had used the rifle earlier that day, there was no response from the enemy. It was as if the VC believed that the wounded soldier had been hit by a random shot and not picked off from close range. No one heard anything. It had to be some kind of fluke.

Tynan was smiling to himself when an enemy platoon seemed to grow out of the ground. Twenty or twenty-five men stood up and began to move forward, in the direction of Crockett. Seconds later there was another rank up and following the first. Tynan couldn't understand it. The grass was not tall enough or the bushes thick enough to hide that many VC.

The enemy soldiers moved out slowly toward Crockett and then turned to the south so that they were moving to the rallying point of the assault forces. Tynan didn't realize it, but he had just stumbled onto the secret of how the VC were able to avoid the artillery. The next thirty minutes would be critical.

11

They had beaten back two assaults. One of them had carried almost to the redoubt, but the sudden fury of the American firing, joined by the machine guns and grenades, had surprised and confused the VC. They had wavered, and when the last of the claymores, set right at the base of the sandbag wall, had been detonated, the attack broke.

Jones dropped down, sitting with his back against the sandbags. He released the magazine in his M-16 and replaced it with a full one. Then he leaned his head against the wall and breathed deeply once, tasting the rain-thickened air. He heard the continual pop of the 81s as the crews tried to keep flares over the base. Artillery exploded around them but didn't seem to be doing anything to inhibit the VC. Overhead there was the beat of helicopter rotor blades and the roar of jet engines. They were waiting for someone on the ground to identify targets for them.

There was an explosion near the sandbags and someone yelled, almost unnecessarily, "Incoming."

Jones rolled to his stomach and wrapped his arms around his head, his nose stuck in the mud that he could almost taste. There was a bang, a loud, flat, abrupt sound that came from a rocket. He heard shrapnel whistle by, hitting the sandbags, splitting them, and could smell the cordite from the burnt gunpowder. He heard a second whoosh, tried to flatten himself more, and waited for the rocket to hit.

Then came the crump of mortars hitting around him and he listened closely, trying to determine if they were coming closer or moving away. He knew that the mortars would be ineffective because of the mud, and as long as he stayed on the ground the shrapnel wouldn't hit him. They might drop a round on him, but they couldn't get him with the shrapnel.

As the sound of the mortars moved away, Jones got to his knees and peered over the low sandbag wall. Through the veil of rain he could see the flashes as the mortar rounds detonated. He could see nothing else except the vague gray shapes of the bunkers on the line and the men who were crouched near him.

As quickly as it started, the barrage ended and there were bugles and shouts. Jones turned and stared into the night. The mist was becoming lighter, easier to see through, and in the distance he could see two or three companies charging toward them.

Where in the hell do they keep coming from? he wondered. The artillery from three different units was exploding all around, trying to suppress the enemy assault, and they kept finding more people to attack. He heard the sporadic firing from the bunker line as the grunts began shooting. He could see the ruby tracers going out and the emerald-green ones coming. Where in the hell are all the VC coming from?

As the last of the men disappeared in the darkness, Tynan propped his CAR-15 next to a tree and pulled the silenced 9mm automatic. He made sure that he had extra grenades, the safety handles pushed through the gaps in his web gear, before he turned to Sterne and whispered, "I'm going out there. You keep me covered."

Sterne was going to protest and put a hand on Tynan's arm but then said nothing. He nodded, and the gesture was nearly lost in the darkness and the rain.

Tynan crawled forward, out of the trees and over a tiny ridge that marked the decaying dike of an abandoned rice paddy. He slipped into the grass, reaching out with a hand to part it. He could see nothing in front of him and continued to creep forward. He passed the remains of a fifty-five-gallon drum cut apart by some forgotten rice farmer, and over a palm log. For a moment he stopped, listening, but heard only the distant crash of the artillery and the burst of the shells. He came to one of the small bushes and touched one of the branches. It seemed to be drier than it should be, as if it were slowly dying.

Tynan searched the ground around him, using one hand to probe the mud. He wondered why there had been no puddles of water. The rain had poured from an open sky, and an old rice paddy should have retained it. Tynan flattened himself, staring into the night. Suddenly he was uneasy. There was something definitely wrong with the paddy. He cocked the hammer of his 9mm, a round already chambered.

He drew back away from the bush and heard a quiet rustling off to his left. He turned and saw a bush there shaking gently as if caught in a sudden breeze, but Tynan could feel no wind. He froze, turning his attention to the left.

The bush seemed to heave, as if sucking in a great breath of air, and then stopped moving. A shape appeared, was still for a moment, and then grew the rest of the way out of the ground. The man stood up for a moment, crouched, and then stared toward the fire base where the artillery boomed. Then he stepped to the right and disappeared into the short grass there until only a black lump that blended with the paddy was visible. Tynan realized that he had just watched a VC exit either a tunnel or a spider hole.

And then he knew the secret of their success at Crockett. He knew what had been flashing into his mind during the debriefings with Walker and the discussions with Riordan. He knew what he should have been able to see hours earlier. The artillery could saturate the whole area, and unless the shell hit the trapdoor of the tunnel, the odds were that the men crouching inside would survive. And the Americans were not using high explosives, but antipersonnel weapons that exploded into shrapnel and fléchettes designed to kill the enemy soldiers. They were useless against fortifications and bunkers because they weren't designed to destroy them.

The enemy shifted suddenly, getting to his hands and knees so that he could creep farther away from the tunnel, first moving to the north and then turning back to where Tynan lay. The man didn't seem to have seen anything. He had watched the popping of the flares over Crockett for a moment and was checking out the paddy before he called the rest of his men from the tunnel hidden below.

He came straight at Tynan, his eyes on the bush, not looking for an American soldier. He stopped, stared, and then began walking again. At that point, Tynan stood up straight, grabbed the man by the back of the neck, forcing him forward, into the barrel of the nine-millimeter. Tynan pulled the trigger, the sound of the shot muffled by the belly of the VC and the silencer fastened to the pistol.

Blood splashed from the gaping wound. The man stood rigid for a moment, his muscles locked, with only a low moaning in his throat. Then his knees buckled and he fell on his back to the ground, both pale hands pressing into the stomach wound. He rolled to his side, drew his legs up as if trying to press his thighs against his stomach. His eyes were wide and white as if he knew that he was going to die and was suddenly afraid. He didn't shout or scream, just grunted once and died.

Tynan turned immediately and ran back to the trees. He leaped the dike and slid to a halt, next to Sterne. He took a minute to look back, but there was no movement in the paddy. There was no response to the shot.

"Boone, grab a couple of the claymores and set them against the base of the rice paddy. Sterne, you, too."

Tynan was up again and crouched near Duke. "How are you doing?"

"I've been better."

"Can you handle a rifle?" asked Tynan.

"Christ, Lieutenant, I took a round in the side. I can still shoot."

"I want you to use the sniper rifle and pick off anyone you see moving out there. Use as much ammo as you have to. I don't know how long that silencer will last before it blows itself up, but don't worry about it. I'm going to set the rest of the claymores."

He grabbed two of the mines and ran to the edge of the trees. He dropped to the ground, aimed the weapon, bracing it against the largest tree, and then backed away, feeding out the wire that would trigger the mine. He set the second twenty feet from the first and wired it. Then he moved to the position he would hold in the trees, setting the controls in front of him so that he knew which one fired which mine. He shrugged his way out of one of the bandoliers and took the magazines from it. He placed several grenades next to the ammo for his CAR-15. Then he got out one of his canteens and drank deeply. He couldn't finish all the water, so he poured the remainder out, not wanting to have it sloshing inside the canteen if he had to try to sneak clear of the area.

Sterne and Boone had finished their work and were moving back into the trees. He could barely see them moving through the light rain. Tynan now had his men on line facing into the paddy, with Duke anchoring the far leg. He heard a soft cough as Duke's silenced M-14 fired once.

Then he saw a dozen men in the rice paddy. Tynan raised his silenced nine-millimeter, fired, missed, and fired again. He grabbed the weapon in both hands to steady it, pointed it at one of the shapes that were springing up all around, and pulled the trigger. There was a loud burp from the weapon and pieces of cotton from the silencer exploded into the sky. He reached around and took the silencer from the barrel and tossed it away. He aimed again but didn't fire because the enemy had yet to react. Out of the corner of his eye, he saw Sterne rise up and throw a grenade. It exploded a moment later, and the targets disappeared as the enemy dropped to the ground.

An AK-47 opened fire. Tynan saw the muzzle flashes and watched the green tracers, but the enemy soldier didn't know where the Americans were hidden. He was just spraying bullets around.

Sterne grabbed another grenade and threw it at the muzzle flashes. It detonated in a roar and a fountain of sparks, and a scream from the man firing.

It was as if a dam had broken then. Firing erupted all over the rice paddy, but the enemy still didn't know where Tynan and his men were hidden. They hosed down the trees, the bushes to the west of the paddy, the open ground around them, trying to find Tynan. They tossed Chicom grenades into the trees, but they were too far from Tynan and his men to do any damage. Several of them failed to explode.

They just kept their heads down, waiting and watching. The firing tapered off and Tynan could hear voices speaking Vietnamese, some seeming to shout orders, others asking questions that weren't answered. He knew that the enemy was organizing his troops to begin a sweep through the whole area. As soon as a man stood or otherwise exposed himself, Tynan cranked off a shot, the sound from the 9mm automatic uncommonly loud compared to the noise the weapon had made when silenced.

Immediately a couple of AKs opened fire, shooting into the trees near Tynan. But no one had seen the muzzle flash, and they were trying to shoot at the sound. They missed by quite a distance.

At the other end of the line, Duke used the silenced M-14, and for a moment that kept the enemy off balance. Sterne and Boone kept lofting grenades into the paddy, the explosions from them masking some of the noise made by Tynan's pistol. Suddenly the firing from the VC weapons became directed. They had finally spotted one of the muzzle flashes from Duke. There was shouting in Vietnamese and four or five men leaped up to attack, but a grenade landed near them, dropping them all into the paddy.

In the distance, just outside the area where the perimeter wire had been, Jones could see a little movement. The flares over Crockett kept the ground dimly lighted, but their oscillating under the parachutes made the shadows shift and shimmer, creating the illusion of movement. He pumped a couple of rounds out anyway.

Then suddenly the VC were on their feet, rushing past the destroyed bunker line, firing their weapons and screaming. Shooting from the grunts erupted. Red tracers crisscrossing with the green and white of the enemy. Fountains of sparks mushrooming as grenades exploded. Yellow flashes from the muzzles of the AK-47s and plumes of pointed fire from the M-60 machine guns.

The attack carried beyond the ruined command bunker, past the bodies of the dead Vietnamese and American soldiers, to the very edge of the sandbag redoubt.

Jones got to his knees, then to his feet, still crouched, still firing, but ready for the enemy when they tried to leap the wall. The first VC there stumbled as he tried to leap, and Jones shot him in the chest, nearly blowing a lung out his back.

The next soldier jumped cleanly to the top of the sandbags, and Jones swung the butt of his rifle at the man. The lightweight plastic of the M-16 stock bounced harmlessly off the VC's side as he sprang forward at Jones.

Jones reached up, as if trying to catch the man, but let the momentum carry through, rolling to his back and pushing with his arms. The VC was flipped, landing flat on his back. Jones scrambled up and around, clawing at the holster of his forty-five. He put a round in the top of the enemy's head. He then spun, facing the wall, and saw more of the VC. He emptied his pistol as fast as he could pull the trigger, killing or wounding five more.

He punched the release for the magazine and let it drop to the ground. Before he could grab a loaded one, another VC leaped the wall, head down and bayonet extended. Jones took a step back and turned so that his left side was pointed at the enemy. He held his hands up, the right one holding his pistol, as if to protect his head, face, and throat.

The enemy halted, braced himself, and feinted with his bayonet, trying to draw Jones's attention to it. He skipped a step and lunged.

Jones had been ready for that. He twisted his body, sucking in his stomach unconsciously. With his left hand he tried to grab the barrel of the rifle, pushing the bayonet away from his body. He drew his right hand back and swung with all his might for the VC's head. The enemy soldier tried to duck, and Jones hit him in the chin. He heard a snapping of bone as the jaw broke and teeth splintered. There was a gurgling scream from the enemy as he let go of the AK and fell.

Jones dropped his forty-five and flipped the AK around, using the bayonet himself. He jabbed it into the chest of the screaming man, silencing him.

The bayonet stuck, and Jones pulled the trigger so that the weapon jerked itself free. He turned back to the wall, suddenly aware of all the noise around. Firing from the individual weapons, hammering from the machine guns, explosions from the grenades, the pop of the mortars, and the crash of the howitzers. Men were screaming in pain, screaming orders, screaming in terror. A roar that seemed to grow and grow as more men entered the battle trying to kill the enemy all around them.

Another enemy jumped to the top of the wall, balanced there precariously, and leveled his weapon at Jones. Jones leaped toward the man, slapped the barrel of the enemy's AK to the side, and fired once. The man fell backward, off the sandbags.

Jones turned in time to see another of the VC. He swung his weapon, but another GI stepped in the way, swinging a heavy ammo can, bringing it down on the top of the VC's head. There was a crunching of bone as the corner of the can smashed through the enemy's pith helmet.

Jones dropped to one knee and, firing from the hip, raked the top of the sandbag wall. He saw a couple of VC topple from it, falling backward, disappearing behind it. From the left a VC charged him and Jones fell to his right side, his AK pointed at the man. He pulled the trigger and watched as the enemy dropped without a sound.

Just as he began to wonder how much longer he could live with the enemy swarming all around, a new sound pierced the battle. A shrill, high-pitched sound that pulsated. It came again and again until the VC started to retreat, started to fall back, away from the redoubt. They stopped shooting and turned to run, their recall still sounding.

Jones jumped forward to the waist-high sandbag wall and watched as the enemy soldiers fled. He aimed a couple of shots after them but didn't seem to hit anyone. As he lowered his rifle he noticed that the firing was tapering off all along the line, except for the machine guns which kept hammering and hammering until only the .50s, with a range of more than two miles, were being used. Finally they, too, fell silent and the only noise was the periodic pop of the mortars firing their illumination rounds and the voices of men calling for help, calling for the medic, or calling for their mothers.

The attack was well coordinated and would have worked if it hadn't been for the claymore mines. Tynan touched his off, raking the VC with a curtain of steel that killed and maimed them. Those not killed or wounded disappeared into the grass.

Tynan had heard the sound of heavy firing at Crockett and had watched through the thinning mist and disappearing cloud cover as the flares blossomed, fell, and were replaced. As long as the flares were overhead, Tynan knew that the Americans still held the fire-support base. As long as he could still hear firing from that direction, he knew that the VC had been unable to take the camp.

Moments later, the firing in the distance seemed to taper and die as if a huge attack had been repelled. Tynan believed it had been repelled, because the flares still burned. He didn't know why Jones didn't contact him by radio.

Before he could worry about it too much, there was renewed firing from the rice paddy and a new group of enemy rushed forward. Tynan tossed his grenades and then grabbed his CAR-15, firing it on full automatic, sweeping the rice paddy with a concentrated fire, the red tracers bouncing high as they ricocheted. He didn't worry about the enemy finding his position; they already knew where he was.

The men with him did the same, firing their rifles as fast as they could reload them. The VC attack wavered and broke, but firing erupted from all around. Tynan tried to melt into the ground, his weapon still firing at the enemy. He burned through five magazines quickly.

To the east he could see the first faint blush of the sun and wondered if he would survive long enough to see it rise. He snapped his attention back to the rice paddy, used the last of his grenades, and then waited. Waited for the VC to swarm over his position and kill him.

The enemy didn't mount another attack. They fired into the trees, their green tracers stripping leaves and bark from them, showering it on Tynan and his men. They threw Chicom grenades that failed to explode or were picked up and thrown back at the VC to detonate there among the enemy. Tynan shot at them, now slowly, firing at the flashes of the enemies' weapons. He would shoot, wait a moment, see another flash, and try to put a round or two right into the center of it. The firing on both sides became sporadic and ineffective.

Around him the others used their rifles or tossed grenades. There would be the explosion of a grenade, screams from the wounded and moans from the dying, and then a few rifle shots. Each side seemed to probe the other with only an occasional bullet.

Just as Tynan realized that the VC was holding his attention to the front and began to worry about a flanking maneuver, the shooting seemed to dry up. Tynan was suddenly aware that he could see more than black shapes against a dark gray background. The sun was rising, giving him the advantage.

Then Tynan realized how the VC could hide a regiment in the area. It had nothing to do with the number of villages or the number of people living there. It was the tunnel system. The Americans could bombard the area for weeks and never penetrate deep enough to destroy the tunnels or kill the VC. They would have to sweep through with a battalion or a brigade, and if they did it soon enough, they could stop the attacks on Crockett. And even if Tynan could no longer see the VC, they were still there, only feet away, but separated from him by the ground and a network of cleverly booby-trapped doors and tunnels.

Tynan waited for a few moments, waited for the VC to do something, to mount another attack, but they didn't. It was getting to be too late in the day. Too much light for the American Air Force and helicopter gunships. Too much light for the American infantry units that would have support from a hundred helicopters. If the VC tried to maneuver in the day, they would be spotted and cut to ribbons. They had gone to ground to wait for the dark.

Tynan leaped to his feet, ran to the other end of the line to check on Duke. The big man lay on his side, a pool of blood near him. He had taken two more hits, either of which could have killed him. There was a bullet hole in the front of his jungle fatigues surrounded by a wet stain of blood. And there was a single hole under his left eye. Tynan could see no exit wound and wondered if the slug had entered Duke's brain or if it had somehow found its way down into his body. Not that it made any difference to Duke. Tynan reached down and pried the M-14 from the dead man's fingers and then looked up at Boone.

"Get on the radio and get us some chopper support," he ordered. "Tell them that we were in contact but have broken it. Tell them we have one dead and no wounded."

"Yes, sir," said Boone, looking at Duke's body. He wanted to say more but couldn't think of a thing that would sound sincere. It all sounded trite and meaningless.

12

The helicopter ride to Crockett was short. The crew chief had helped them load Duke's body. They had been unable to wrap it in a poncho liner because they hadn't brought one into the field with them. They just laid him on the floor of the cargo compartment, stretched out as if he were asleep, except that there were the ragged, rust-colored stains on his fatigues and his face was white, nearly translucent, as if all the blood had drained away. The only blemish was the small hole with the bruised edges under his eye.

Jones met them at the helicopter landing area. He got two grunts to carry the body over to where the rest of the American dead waited to be evacked.

Tynan stepped down out of the helicopter and held up a hand to shield his eyes in the bright morning sun. The base was a ruin. Fires burned everywhere. Every structure had been damaged and a number had been destroyed. Several of them still smoked where fires had only recently been extinguished. Dead lay everywhere. Hundreds of dead. Dead wearing the OD jungle fatigues of the Americans, the black pajamas of the VC, and the khaki of the NVA. He wanted to talk to Riordan but no longer knew where to find the colonel.

"Where's Riordan?" asked Tynan.

"Wounded. Bunker collapsed on him," said Jones. "He was evacked out at first light."

"Who's in command?"

"Major Quinn." Jones turned and looked toward the ruined command bunker. "The last time I saw him, he was working over there."

"Thanks," said Tynan. He started to move in that direction but stopped and looked at Jones. "You okay?"

Jones's fatigues were crusted with dried mud and blood. One sleeve was torn and a pocket was flapping in the breeze. He had lost his helmet. There were dark circles under his eyes and a giant bruise, just beginning to discolor, on the side of his face. Somebody's blood had splattered his chest, up onto his neck and the side of his face. His light blond hair hung in his eyes, and he was sweating heavily. He looked as if he would be sick at any moment.

He grinned uneasily. "I'm fine, especially if we can get out of here."

"I think we'll be out of here by noon. At the very latest." Tynan turned and headed toward the remains of the command bunker. Through the doorway he could see bright light, which meant that part of the roof had caved in. He stepped around the sandbag wall that protected the entrance. Some of it had toppled over, leaving the top of it ragged and uneven. The sandbags were ripped and leaking.

Tynan looked through the doorway and saw that one wall had partially collapsed and a large section of the roof, beams and sandbags, had cascaded to the wooden floor. The table and chairs he had seen his first time in the bunker were smashed, and he could see no sign of the radios. Two men were slowly picking up the sandbags and tossing them to the side as if searching for something buried under them. They were too busy to notice that Tynan had entered.

Then, to his right, standing outside the bunker, he saw a large man with black hair giving orders to an NCO. Tynan approached and asked, "Major Quinn?"

The man with the black hair turned. He had a pale face with a long nose and bright blue eyes. There was a thick black stubble that reached from his pointed chin nearly to his eyes. He was a big man, standing nearly six four, and had a barrel chest. Quinn was wearing a flak jacket that was torn in several places, and Tynan could see a ragged chunk of shrapnel embedded in it over Quinn's hip. There was a blood-stain on the front, but Tynan could see no sign of an injury to Quinn. There was mud nearly covering him, and his steel pot was badly dented as if it had taken a glancing hit from an AK round.

"I'm Quinn."

"Tynan. I was in the field last night."

Quinn dismissed the sergeant with a nod and an instruction. "You get that done first." Then, to Tynan, he said, "I've been waiting for you. Riordan said that you would probably come in today. Didn't really say what the fuck you were doing out there last night but said that you had a couple of ideas. We've got to figure something out for tonight, otherwise we're going to lose Crockett."

"Don't worry about it, Major," said Tynan. "I think I've got your answer. Is there somewhere we can talk?"

"I think the mess hall survived in pretty good shape. Let's go over there and I'll buy you a cup of coffee. Providing we still have cups, coffee, and something to brew it in. I don't know what we've got left after last night."

The mess hall hadn't survived all that well. One corner had been blown out, the sandbags and supporting wood structures lying in the pools of water left by the heavy rain. The screen door had been shredded and hung by the top hinge. Inside, the big fan had lost two blades and the pole it stood on was bent double. The serving area was riddled with bullets and shrapnel. There was a crater in the floor where someone had tossed a grenade. Tables had been upended, the legs broken from some of them. Others had been hit by rifle fire. Chairs were scattered and debris littered the floor. Quinn stooped and picked up a C-ration can of peaches. He stared at the black printing on the OD tin, started to set it on a table, and then stuffed it into the front pocket of his flak jacket.

Quinn pointed to a table that was standing upright. "Have a seat. I'll see if I can find any coffee, although I think the cooks are all outside working on the perimeter. We've got everyone outside working on the perimeter."

"Doesn't matter," said Tynan.

Quinn dropped into the chair opposite Tynan. "No, I guess it doesn't. Now, what did you find?" He leaned forward, both hands supporting his chin. His eyes closed as if he had gone to sleep in seconds.

Tynan detailed his night in the field so that Quinn would understand what he had seen and the significance of it. He mentioned that they had watched the enemy forces form for the assaults. He told of the hiding places they had found and the rally points they had discovered. He talked of the ability of the VC to conceal themselves in rice paddies and forests around Crockett. He went into great detail, outlining everything so that Quinn would get the whole picture. He wanted Quinn to understand what he was saying before he got to the point.

Finally he added, "We were having trouble finding the major concentrations of the enemy troops. We would circulate out there, find a good ambush site, and wait. The VC would soon appear, but we never really saw them infiltrating. They would just be there. I think the majority of them are underground. In a tunnel system."

Quinn merely nodded at that as if he didn't understand and was listening to be polite. But he became lost in thought. "Tunnels!" he snapped suddenly. "Of course. They're in the fucking tunnels, and that makes our artillery ineffective. And our air strikes. And everything else we do. They just sit down there, probably cool and comfortable, waiting for nightfall so that they can storm the wire."

"Yes, sir," said Tynan. "But put an infantry brigade into the field, and they'll never be able to mount an attack. You can just sit back and pick them off as they come out."

"Which gives the initiative to the enemy," said Quinn.

"With the infantry," said Tynan, "you can go get them. You don't have to wait for them. Sweep through the paddies and trees and drop grenades down the entrances. You can probably disrupt them enough to keep them from attacking tonight."

Quinn was on his feet. "Tynan, you've done a hell of a job. If you had done nothing else, this one piece of information would have made your contribution significant. I've got to get on the horn and talk to people. I've got to get that brigade we talked about." He held out a hand. "Thanks."

Tynan watched Quinn rush from the mess hall. He leaned back in the chair, laced his hands behind his head, and thought, That's it. We've done it, and Quinn will be able to hold the base now.

* * *

Tynan didn't know what Quinn did, but within an hour the skies around the fire-support base were filled with helicopters. Some of them landed at the helipad, but the majority circled to the north of the camp as Quinn or one of his officers directed traffic. From the insignia on the front of the choppers, Tynan could tell that Quinn had gotten the support of units from all over III Corps. He could see the Hornets, the Crusaders, the Tomahawks, and the Raiders. There were helicopters from the Deans, the 25th Infantry Division, and the 1st Air Cav.

The 105s were firing almost continuously. Periodically one of the companies of helicopters would break from the massive formation, dive to the ground, and disappear for several minutes. In the silence between the crashing of the artillery, Tynan could hear machine-gun fire in the distance. He could see the gun platoons of the various assault helicopter units working the tree lines or the rice paddies south and west of Crockett. They were using 2.75-inch rockets and miniguns, which would be useless against troops hiding in tunnels but devastating against men in the open.

Tynan sat on a stack of sandbags, one hand shading his eyes, watching the show. In his mind he could visualize what was happening. A scout ship would spot something on the ground: a flash of movement, an enemy soldier, or evidence that someone had been in the area. Artillery would be called in to soften the LZ, to detonate any booby traps that the VC might have laced through the clearing, or to destroy enemy bunkers. When the arty prep finished, one of the assault helicopter companies, ten aircraft carrying seven or eight Americans each, would swoop in, door guns blazing. They would touch down, the grunts would leap to the ground and sweep into the trees. But now they would be looking for evidence of spider holes and tunnel entrances. They would be searching for vegetation that didn't quite match the surroundings, vegetation that was a little too dry, and when they found that, they would use explosives to destroy the tunnel entrance.

From all that Tynan had learned in the last few hours about the VC tunnel complexes in the area, he knew that they would never be able to clear them all. The whole of the Hobo Woods was laced with tunnels. There were sleeping quarters, hospitals, factories, arms lockers, and anything else that a military base needed buried there. The VC had built false tunnels that were booby-trapped. They had built false walls that concealed the real tunnels. There were miles of them that went a hundred feet into the ground. Two hundred feet. And they were so well constructed that the artillery and bombs from the Air Force couldn't collapse them.

But with the infantry on the ground, tossing satchel charges into the tunnels and forcing the VC to either fight or flee, the enemy couldn't coordinate the attack. Too many Americans were now in the area. Too many Americans who knew what to look for. And too many Americans would be in the field that night. Charlie would not be able to form his units. All he could do was fade from sight.

It was late in the afternoon when Tynan and his men were told that they should catch a flight out. Quinn came by to thank him again. He stood for a moment, his steel pot pushed back on his head. He held out a hand and said, "I don't know what we would have done tonight. Charlie had shot us up pretty bad. I think he might have been able to overrun the base if we hadn't found his rally points."

Tynan was unsure of what to say. He thought about the three men who had died. He thought about the nights in the field and the piece of information that had seemed trivial at first but that had taken on such importance. He took Quinn's hand and shook it and said, "I'm sure that you would have held."

"Maybe. Maybe not. Anyway, thanks for the help, and if there is anything we can do for you, let me know."

"I will." Tynan turned and walked back to the helicopter waiting for him. He climbed on slowly, sat down, and then buckled the seat belt. He felt strange. Tired. Depressed. He didn't know why. Maybe it was because the assignment was over and he could see nothing on the horizon except trouble with Walker. Or maybe it was because three of his men had died. He still hadn't dealt with that, or writing the letters to the families at home. Maybe those letters would focus his emotions better. Right now he had no real thoughts about it.

The flight to Nha Be seemed to be nearly instantaneous. Tynan suddenly found himself climbing out of the chopper without a memory of how he had gotten there. Standing at the head of the dock was Walker, another commander, and an admiral. Behind them was a small Navy band, and to one side was a color guard. As soon as Tynan's foot hit the ground, the band began playing "Anchors Aweigh."

Tynan moved forward, stood in front of the admiral, and saluted. The band stopped playing and the unidentified commander said, "Attention to orders."

He folded back the papers and said in a loud, clear voice, "By direction of the President of the United States the Silver Star is presented to Lieutenant Mark M. Tynan . . ."

Tynan stood at attention. He didn't listen to the orders. He glanced at Walker, who looked as if he had bitten into something sour. The admiral was grinning. Undoubtedly he had had something to do with the impact award of the Silver Star. Maybe Quinn had too. Tynan wasn't sure that he could believe it.

When the narration ended, the admiral stepped forward, took a small rectangular box from the hand of an aide, and opened it. Inside was the bright red-white-and-blue ribbon and the heavy silver star. He pinned the decoration to the front of Tynan's dirty, sweat-stained fatigues. He shook Tynan's hand and said, "Congratulations, Lieutenant. You deserve this and more."

As the admiral stepped back the commander began reading again, detailing the award of the Bronze Star for valor to Thomas K. Jones. They presented medals to all the members of Tynan's team. Then they announced the presentation of posthumous awards to the men killed. They also received the Purple Heart for wounds received.

When the ceremony was over, the admiral buttonholed Tynan. With Sousa marches blaring in the background, the admiral said, "You did a fine job out there. For the Army to recommend you for a Silver Star is quite impressive, and to have the commander of Three Corps to call to expedite it is nearly impossible to believe."

"Yes, sir," said Tynan.

"Anything that you or your boys want, you let me know. You give me a call. I'll make sure that my yeoman knows the name."

Tynan hesitated and then said, "After we have a chance to clean up, I would like some time in Saigon. Couple of days there for me and my boys."

The admiral laughed. "Ask for something hard. Of course I'll authorize some leave time in Saigon. In fact, take a week. Then report back aboard your ship."

"Commander Walker has some idea about that," said Tynan.

"Not anymore," said the admiral. "Those orders have been rescinded. They were issued before I fully understood what was happening and the nature of your unit. Don't worry about Walker. I'll have a talk with him."

"Yes, sir. Thank you, sir."

Three days later, Tynan sat at a table in the rooftop restaurant of the Oriental Hotel, watching as the civilian employees of the embassy walked in. Bobbi entered with a couple of men in khaki uniforms that were only slightly damp from the afternoon heat. She glanced toward him and he half waved, wanting to get her attention but afraid of attracting the men with her. He wanted to separate her from her companions.

She put a hand on the arm of the taller and said something. He nodded, shot a glance at Tynan, and nodded again. As they walked toward the bar she broke away from them, hurrying toward Tynan. She was wearing a light-colored blouse open at the throat and a skirt that didn't even reach to midthigh. She held up a hand to wave as a grin spread across her face.

When she reached him, she breathed a sexy "Hi" at him as she kissed his cheek. She slipped into the chair closest to him and said, "How you been?" She crossed her legs slowly.

"I wasn't sure that you'd still be happy to see me," said Tynan.

"Now, why would you think that?" she asked. "I missed you greatly. I tried to call you on that ship of yours, but the captain wouldn't tell me a thing. Only that you were not available. God! Is that frustrating!"

Tynan smiled, leaned forward, and kissed her gently on the lips. "Let's go somewhere to celebrate."

She leaped up and said, "Thought you'd never ask. It'll be worth your while too."

It was.

KILLSQUAD

by Frank Garrett

WANTED: A world strike force—the last hope of the free world—the ultimate solution to global terrorism!

THE WEAPON: Six desperate and deadly inmates from Death Row led by the invincible Hangman...

THE MISSION: To brutally destroy the terrorist spectre wherever and whenever it may appear...

KILLSQUAD #1 Counter Attack   75151-8/$2.50 US/$2.95 Can
America's most lethal killing machine unleashes its master plan to subdue the terrorquake planned by a maniacal extremist.

#2 Mission Revenge   75152-6/$2.50 US/$2.95 Can
A mad zealot and his army of drug-crazed acolytes are on the march against America...until they face the Killsquad.

#3 Lethal Assault   75153-4/$2.50 US/$3.50 Can
The Fourth Reich is rising again, until the Hangman rounds up his Death Row soldiers for some hard-nosed Nazi-hunting.

#4 The Judas Soldiers   75154-2/$2.50 US/$3.50 Can
A madman seeks to bring America to its knees with mass doses of viral horror, but Killsquad shows up with its own bloody cure.

#5 Blood Beach   75155-0/$2.50 US/$3.50 Can
The Hangman and his Killer crew go halfway around the world to snuff out a Soviet/Cuban alliance seizing control in Africa.